The Man from

Devil's Island

By G. H. Teed

From The Union Jack magazine,
Series 2, No. 1380, March 29, 1930.

Illustrated by Eric Parker

Stillwoods Edition

Stillwoods.Blogspot.Ca

Catalogue Information
Title: The Man from Devil's Island
Author: G. H. Teed
First published in The Union Jack magazine, Series 2, No. 1380,
March 29, 1930.
Illustrated by Eric Parker
This Edition: Stillwoods, 2020 (Doug Frizzle)
ISBN Canada: 978-1-989788-13-4
Blog: Stillwoods.Blogspot.Ca
Author Blog: http://ghteed.blogspot.com/
Storefront: http://www.lulu.com/spotlight/lulubook22

Keywords: Sexton Blake, British fictional detective, Roxane
Harfield.

A Complete Sexton Blake Detective-Adventure Story.

A story of intrigue and human drama, featuring Sexton Blake and
Mademoiselle Roxane.

A complete story of Sexton Blake, detective, by the popular
author of: They Shall Repay!

Eight men, crooks of commerce, swindled a girl out of her
inheritance and killed her mother as a result. Craftily within the law,
no legal means could touch them. The girl dedicated her life to their
ruin. Widely separated now, she deals with them one by one. This
story tells how she metes out justice to the convict-trader of Devil's
Islands. The girl: Mademoiselle Roxane.

Roxane Harfield

Roxane Harfield, a heroine and villain in Sexton Blake stories, was born in New Brunswick, Canada, is featured in these stories. Her knowledge of the New Brunswick South-East shoreline, and Bay of Fundy, is a key feature of many of these thrillers from USA prohibition days.

Many of these stories use locales in Canada.

A Chronology of G. H. Teed and **Roxanne** work in:

"The Union Jack"

No.

In bold means available at my bookstore, others in progress /drf

What follows is a beginning chronology of Teed's **Roxanne Harfield** stories. It is a quotation from Black Spaniard Creek (p10).

"There were some persons—Sexton Blake the famous English detective, among them—who before that trial knew something of the story of Roxane Harfield, and how those same men, together with the one now dead, had defrauded her and her mother out of the lumber property in the Province of New Brunswick, which had been the sole legacy from her father, John Harfield; knew how the shock of the discovery had sent the mother to her death; and knew how the girl, almost penniless but full of staunch courage, had set herself to prosecute a vendetta against these eight men.

And fewer knew how she had succeeded. In court the story came out— how she had befooled one, Harold Carruthers, by working as his own private secretary for three years while learning the inmost secrets of his operations on the Montreal Stock Exchange, had speculated on her own account until she had built up a comfortable capital, and then, at a time when Carruthers counted on every penny he could swing for a big deal, had cleaned him out of every penny, leaving him stranded, a drugged, gibbering wreck, in the streets of London.

They learned how she had bought and fitted out one of the most luxurious oil-burning yachts that ever came off the slips of Camper & Nickerson's yards; how she had picked a trustworthy crew, and had sailed to French Guiana, where she had exacted vengeance upon a second member of the syndicate—one Chris Henley.

Then the romantic story of how she had proceeded to Saigon, in French Indo-China, to deal a hammer-blow at still a third—Digby Farren. Of her quiet arrival on the Malabar Coast of India, to wreak a terrible punishment upon Stillman Pearce, whose downfall was made all the easier through his mad infatuation for her beauty.

Followed the hunting out of Marius Lagran, who, while ostensibly engaged in selling cigars in a shop in Piccadilly, was, in reality, running a big diamond swindle. Lagran had been shot dead in a terrible battle with Sexton Blake and a man who had been Lagran's partner years before, who had been swindled and deserted by Lagran.

Then out of the narrowing list of names came a titanic struggle with Louis Martinel, one of the former leading spirits of the gang; and, later, engaged in timber speculation in many parts of eastern and northern Canada. There, as with the others, Roxane had been victorious.

And, lastly, there had been the comparatively easy ruining of Gus Hovey in London, and the far more difficult matter of dealing with Felix Dupont, who had settled in Paris, and who had as assistant a girl who was almost as capable, quite as beautiful, and in some ways more sophisticated than Roxane— Sophie Beautemps.

In all of these affairs Sexton Blake had taken a hand because, in one way and another, they had crossed cases upon which he was engaged. Towards the end, when Felix Dupont would have joined his name with that of Roxane in a scandal, Blake had taken open sides with the girl, and no one would have acknowledged more readily than Roxane that it was really due to Blake that six of the seven still alive had been put behind prison bars."

Cautionary Note: This series of books by Stillwoods are intended to make the stories of G. H. Teed, born in New Brunswick Canada, available to collectors and researchers. The editor, or rather digitizer has not altered the original publication.

This story may contain language and racial terms that are not appropriate to today. I apologize for them; I know that the author was using his voice to excite an adventurous English audience. These works were published from 82 to 110 years ago. Most every work has characters of redeeming ethnicity within.

I hope you enjoy and share these stories; I have.

Doug Frizzle

The MAN from DEVIL'S

The Second Officer leaned over and tried to draw the man to the boat's side. Emitting a hoarse croak, he began threshing about, resisting.

ISLAND — by G.H.Teed

A complete story of Sexton Blake, detective, by the popular author of: They Shall Repay!

Chapter 1. The Man Who Swam.

ROXANE HARFIELD came on deck just as the eastern sky was spreading its pink streamers to herald the coming day.

The trim, powerful yacht, La Brise, caught the light and blushed rosily as if, like some shy maiden, she had been surprised in the chaste robes of her chamber; the brasswork gleamed golden where it caught the fire from the east.

Off to starboard lay the coast of French Guiana, the dense forests of the hinterland banking away in heavy, sinister purple. For untold leagues along the coast to the north, and for more untold leagues to the south was the same vast, unknown forest—the almost impenetrated and untapped natural domain that stretches from Colombia and Venezuela south through the vast basins of the Orinoco and the Amazon, with black tentacles of jungle thrown out to embrace the three wedges in the South American coast that make the three Guianas—British, French, and Dutch.

Ever since the ship had left Georgetown, Barbados, the sea had been like glass, and now, as the owner, Roxane Harfield, stood just outside the wide companion, a very spirit of the morning herself, the girl gazed to right and left. The water appeared of the consistency of oil.

"We are in for another scorcher," she murmured as she strolled to the side and nodded smilingly to a sailor who was just finishing a bit of holystoning. Then she waved a greeting to Cameron, the second officer, on the bridge. She was about to lean against the port rail and drink in the morning freshness when she heard his voice.

"Would you mind coming up here, Miss Roxane? There is something I'd like you to see."

"All right. Mr. Cameron—coming."

The second, a youngish man in the early thirties, sturdy, dark, and clear of eye, watched her with an expression that could only be described as devoted.

In fact, there wasn't a man on board the yacht La Brise who wouldn't have given his life for the young owner. She treated them with extraordinary kindness and generosity, but, nevertheless, admitted no one to greater intimacy than another, unless it might be Captain Foster, who had passed his sixtieth year. But even with him her word was law, and once she had issued an order there was no questioning its purport.

Implicit obedience and a closed month, utter loyalty and unquestioned courage were the chief essentials to a job on the yacht La Brise, and officers and crew counted themselves lucky that they had succeeded in measuring up to the required standard.

Before mounting the companion to the bridge the young owner lit a cigarette; then, as she topped the ladder:

"What is it, Mr. Cameron? I hope you have something exciting to show me. To tell you the truth, I am getting a little bored."

"I don't think it is much, Miss Roxane, but it puzzles me a bit. Will you take these glasses and focus them as I shall show you. No, not there—a little more to the right. That should be about it. Do you see anything?"

Roxane turned the thumbscrew a little to get the focus better for her sight, and then as she looked she saw a tiny black speck on the oily surface of the water, a little blob that seemed to move over so slowly and, at intervals of a second or so, to be accompanied by smaller blobs, one on either side. She studied the object for some moments before lowering the glasses.

"There certainly is something on the surface, Mr. Cameron. It looks almost like someone swimming—if one could imagine such a thing in these shark-infested waters a good three miles or more from the land."

The second nodded as he fixed the glasses once more on the spot.

"Just what I thought," he said. "And the more I look at it, Miss Roxane, the more convinced I am that it is someone swimming—impossible as it may seem. What puzzles me is why should he be swimming seawards? If it is some nigger who has been tumbled out of his skiff or someone who has fallen overboard from some passing schooner, why is he heading this way? It is a mystery to me why the sharks haven't got him before now—if it is a man."

"Maybe it's a manatee," suggested Roxane mischievously.

"Or a mermaid," he countered in response to his employer's mood. "Please take another look, Miss Roxane. If it is a man I suppose we'd better do something about it?"

She glanced at him sharply.

"You really do think it is? Let me look. I am afraid I was not taking you very seriously."

Swiftly she trained the glasses once more, and now, as she gazed, a little pucker marred her broad, white brow. She spoke while still gazing at the moving object, and now one might have noticed that where, before, her voice had held a hint of raillery in it, it was now crisp and businesslike.

"You are right I should say, Mr. Cameron. It looks very much like a human being. Alter your course at once, and come round so we can make sure. Then be ready to lower away a boat."

"Very good, miss."

He strode along the deck and gave the necessary orders to the quartermaster at the wheel; then he sent a hail forward and snapped further orders for a boat to be swung outboard. Then he rejoined Roxane, who handed him the glasses silently.

WHILE the second was again watching the moving speck, commenting on its progress from time to time while Roxane puffed at her cigarette, they were joined by Captain Foster, looking spruce and ruddy from bath and razor; his white duck uniform spotless and almost dazzling in the morning light. He saluted his owner meticulously, took Cameron's salute, and glanced quizzically at the glasses.

"What have you found of interest, Mr. Cameron?"

"It looks like a man swimming, sir. Will you give us your opinion?"

The skipper took the binoculars and swung them with a practised hand. Though past sixty, his blue eyes were as clear as a young man's, and so trained to the vagaries of the seven seas, and so accustomed to many weird forms of flotsam and jetsam that he was much quicker at appraising a thing than his younger officers. It was no fault of his that he had lost his ship in a typhoon off Formosa, but it had cost him his ticket, and not even Roxane knew how his heart swelled with gratitude to her when he surveyed the lovely yacht that was now his charge; the daintiest little thing that could come out of the builder's hands— the snuggest berth one could want in the autumn of life.

"It is a man," he announced, after a quick scrutiny of the speck. "I see you have already altered the course, Mr. Cameron. Your orders, ma'am?"

"Yes, captain. Are you sure it is a man swimming?"

"Not a doubt. I've seen enough heads bobbing on the sea not to make a mistake. Will you look, ma'am?"

"I have already done so. But why should a man be swimming out to sea, Captain Foster? If he has fallen overboard off some craft why isn't he making for the shore?"

"There are two reasons I can think of, ma'am. One is because he wants to get away from the shore, the other is because he is in such a befuddled state he doesn't know in what direction he is swimming."

"If that is the case, then he can't have seen us."

"No, ma'am. But if he is swimming because he wants to got away from the land, then he isn't caring very much whether he is picked up or not. It won't be the first time a man has swum into the horizon from that coast, ma'am."

A sombre look came into Roxane's eyes. She knew what the skipper meant. He was referring to the fact that the coast they were passing was that of French Guiana, off which lies the group of islands known by the name of one of them—Devil's Island, of terrible and evil notoriety. Yet on the mainland itself were thousands of one-time convicts, effectively imprisoned by the surrounding jungle and conditions made by man, in a state of so-called freedom, dragging through an existence of unspeakable degradation and suffering.

Was this speck on the water, then, one of those poor devils who was seeking to swim into the restfulness of death?

By this time the yacht had swung round in a great semicircle, so that they could now easily distinguish the moving object with the naked eye. There could be no doubt now that it was a human being, but if he was aware of the approach of succour he gave no sign, swimming on steadily, as if he were heading straight along the path that the rising sun had laid on the water, as if he would go on and on until he was swallowed up in that great orb of forgetfulness.

"I'll take the bridge, Mr. Cameron," she heard Captain Foster say. "Take charge of the boat."

"Ay, ay, sir!"

The second swung down the ladder to the deck. The crew that had been chosen climbed in. The boat was lowered away, and then shot off towards the moving speck.

Even now the swimmer did not pause or change is course. Nor, strangely enough, was there any sign of sharks in waters which were notorious for them. He just kept on moving his arms mechanically, making slow progress.

Roxane and the skipper watched while the boat drew near. The yacht's engines had been stopped, and they were running ahead at a steadily decreasing speed under their own impetus. So close were they it was quite easy to hear Cameron's hail. But still the swimmer paid not the slightest heed.

It was strange, uncanny. It seemed to be a case of unwilling suicide.

Then the watchers saw the dinghy draw in close, saw Cameron stand up and lean over towards the man in the water. They could hear the sound of his voice as he spoke sharply twice, then narrowed their eyes to see more clearly as he tried to catch hold of the swimmer and drag him to the side.

It was as if the other had become aware for the first time that any other humans were close to him. Emitting a hoarse croak, he began threshing about like a madman, his croak rising to a scream.

Roxane snatched up the glasses and focused them. The face she saw would remain in her memory to her dying day—wide, terror-stricken eyes, a gaping mouth showing red against a face that was matted with a tangled beard. She watched the terrible struggle till she could stand it no longer, then laid the glasses down, and, feeling somewhat sick, touched Captain Foster on the arm.

"I am going below." she said in a low tone. "Come to me later and tell me what it means."

Chapter 2.   The Liberated One.

ROXANE HARFIELD sat writing at the unpolished walnut desk in the small saloon of the yacht when Captain Foster presented himself.

It was mid-morning, and, as usual, Roxane was engaged with her accounts or correspondence. Immediately after breakfast it was her custom to devote three hours to this work; then, at eleven, a cup of chocolate and an interview with her captain regarding the affairs of the yacht.

Her life, ever since she had set herself to a certain purpose, had been as rigidly apportioned in its duties as that of the most iron-willed captain of industry.

From the day when, as a young girl at the Harfield camp in the woods of New Brunswick, she had gazed upon the still form of her mother, and realised that death had come through the swindling machinations of eight men who, having been shareholders in her father's timber companies during his lifetime, had thus gained her and her mother's confidence, she had sworn a vow to be avenged upon them for the thing they had done. She had worked for that thing, and that only.

Five years it had taken her to prepare herself to fight. In those five years she had taken the few thousand dollars that had been left to her by the human wolves and had devoted herself to a study of the share market in Montreal. In a small way at first, then more and more boldly, she had played the market until, during one big bull movement, she had amassed more than a million dollars.

With that as her "war chest" she disguised herself as a prim and frigid spinster, and after six months' more patient work succeeded in getting into the offices of one, Harold Carruthers as typist.

She had chosen Carruthers first for the simple reason that he was one of the leading spirits in the deal that had swindled her so tragically, and, further, because he had come in person with one of the other eight to make sure that their plan would succeed.

How well she succeeded in gaining his confidence, fighting him secretly in the stock market, and eventually plotting his complete ruin, has already been told. Sufficient is it to say that, although he was left a broken and ruined man, Roxane did not hold the sixty thousand pounds which she had taken. It was due to the famous detective,

Sexton Blake, that this money found another keeper; but in that first clash between Blake and Roxane a flame had been lit that was to have far-reaching and drastic effects before it was even dimmed.

It may have been that she was thinking something of the sort as she sat at her desk toying with a pencil, for the figures she had been scrawling on a pad of paper for some time were quite meaningless. Be that as it may, her eyes were hazy in expression, bore a faraway look of something strangely wistful, when Captain Foster entered, doffed his gold-braided cap, and took the seat he always occupied during these sessions.

"Ring, please, captain!"

Turning, the skipper pressed a button. Immediately a white-jacketed steward appeared, bearing the usual tray of two cups of thick chocolate topped with whipped cream, and a plate of biscuits. When the steward had gone and Roxane had taken a sip of the chocolate, she looked up at her skipper. For the thousandth time that individual found himself gazing helplessly into the lovely violet eyes that now smiled into his. She was very beautiful and very desirable, was this young owner of his, from her russet-crowned head to the tips of her silken-clad toes.

"Well," she said in the husky tones that were such a fascinating quality of her voice, "what about our swimmer? How is he now?"

"Ma'am, I'm puzzled about that man. He was clean loony, if you will pardon my expression, when he was brought aboard. He is calmer now and I have had him bathed, and shaved. In clean clothes he looks a different person, ma'am, but unless I'm mistaken he has been through hell, begging your pardon."

"The word is a proper description of some forms of suffering," she responded. "What do you make of him? Why was he swimming out to sea?"

"I've got some sort of sense out of him, ma'am, but I don't know if it is the truth. He won't stand being pressed—breaks down and cries like a baby. Something had torn pretty close to his soul, ma'am, if you understand what I mean."

"I think I do understand," she answered, in a low, sombre tone. "Was he trying to find death?"

Captain Foster hesitated. Then he took what seemed a plunge.

"Ma'am, it isn't for me to speak of your reason for coming to this accursed country. It is enough for me to know what your orders are.

But you have honoured me, ma'am, with your confidence, and I know you expect to find a certain person here."

"Quite right. Captain Foster. What bearing has that on the man we have rescued?"

"You will recall, ma'am, back in Marseilles after that affair when we —er—"

She smiled faintly.

"You mean when I carried out my purpose against Harold Carruthers and kidnapped the British detective, Sexton Blake? Yes, I recall quite well our conversation in Marseilles after we landed Sexton Blake and his young assistant in Tangier. We talked at some length, I believe, of French Guiana and the penal settlement here. In fact, that was my reason for putting into Marseilles, even at some risk of unpleasant inquiries on the part of the police. I wanted certain books and official records about this dumping-ground of criminals. I got them, and I learned a little more about the person whom I had heard was in French Guiana. But you yourself told me more than the books, captain."

"That's what I'm getting at, ma'am. I told you about the prisoners on Devil's Island, for I know something about that purgatory. And I also explained about the incorrigibles they call the "relegues," and the ex-convicts that are known as "liberes.""

"I remember perfectly."

"Well, ma'am, this young fellow we picked up claims to be a libere. He stood the torture as long as he could, and managed to make a dash for it—found the sea with the gang hot on his heels, and took to the water. I'm telling you this, ma'am, because we are headed for Cayenne and St. Laurent, this minute, and it may mean trouble."

"You mean if it should get winded abroad that we had picked him up, I suppose?"

"Yea, ma'am. You see, we were only about three miles offshore— might have been inside their waters when we actually dragged him over the side. And we may have been watched through glasses. This yacht is one that would stand out among the ordinary craft that pass up and down this coast like a pearl on a garbage heap. There is a risk in it, ma'am."

ROXANE was thoughtful for some minutes. Mechanically she lit a cigarette and puffed slowly. Then at last: "What is your own opinion, captain?"

"I don't like to pass it, ma'am. I will say that he strikes me as a different cut from the usual relegue and libere; but, then, they are the sweepings of the French criminal underworld. But I may be mistaken. If it becomes known to the French authorities in Cayenne or St. Laurent that we picked him up, it might make things very nasty for you, and spoil your plans."

"This fellow is not violent?"

"No; just weak and hysterical."

"Is he fit to be seen if I speak gently to him?"

"Ma'am, a tiger would be gentle if you spoke to him."

Roxane smiled, but shook her head reprovingly.

"No blarneying, captain have him brought along, and I will see what I can get out of him."

"I'll have him brought."

They settled a few matters regarding orders for the day, then the skipper rose and went out. When he was gone Roxane opened a drawer in the desk and took out a snapshot, obviously taken on board the yacht, and showed a man and a youth walking along the deck. The man seemed to be speaking, while the lad was smiling pleasantly.

A clean-cut looking pair they were in their blue serge, with heads bared to the wind. One would scarcely have thought, looking at the photograph, that they were prisoners on board when it was taken, with not a ghost of an idea whither they were bound. But a good many thousands would have recognised them easily enough—Sexton Blake and his assistant, Tinker.

Roxane studied the features of the man for a little; then she shook her head in a puzzled way.

"I wish I understood you," she murmured. "You were, and are, an enigma to me. Why didn't you give in when there wasn't a chance of your escaping? Yet you made a chance. I wonder what you would do in the present circumstances, I wonder—"

Suddenly, as she heard the sound of dull footfalls on the rubber matting outside the saloon, the photograph was popped out of sight.

"It doesn't matter what you would think," she murmured, with a hint of irritation in her voice. "You will never cross my path or my will again."

She little knew how mistaken she was.

"PITIFUL—oh, how pitiful!"

The whispered words dragged from Roxane as she saw the figure that came through the doorway, supported by Captain Foster and Cameron, the second officer.

There was little outward resemblance to the wild-looking creature whom Cameron and his men had dragged out of the water. Then he had been sodden with sea-brine, his face caked with dirt and matted with an unkempt beard, his eyes full of a frenzied terror.

Now he was shaven clean and his mahogany-coloured skin on the cheekbones showed in startling contrast to the white of the chin, side-cheeks and throat, where the hair had been shaved away. He was dressed in white flannels, with a tennis shirt of Cameron's; but even though the second was a man of spare frame the garments hung on him in loose folds.

The man's eyes, dark brown in colour, seemed almost lost in the great hollows of the sockets, and from their depths looked out upon Roxane like those of a captured animal. The skin over the facial bones was drawn tight as parchment, the bones of the hands were startlingly distinct through the taut covering; his mouth was pinched and drawn back until it showed the teeth. If it wasn't a case of starvation, torture, and privation of the worst order, Roxane Harfield had never looked on human suffering.

At the moment of entering, his gaze had become fixed on hers. She smiled kindly upon him and motioned for him to approach. His lips made a convulsive movement as if he were trying to respond to the smile, were struggling to believe that such a wonderful creature as she seemed was not the vision of a maddened brain.

His eyes wandered away from hers, and he quivered from head to foot when Captain Foster and Cameron tried to urge him forward. His gaze travelled about the luxurious fittings of the saloon and through the open glass doors that led out on to the sun veranda. It all troubled him very much. Twelve hours ago he had been in a reeking hell of squalor, filth, and hideousness, and now—this.

He shook his head in a way that brought tears to Roxane's eyes.

"Pitiful," she breathed again. "What, dear Heaven, what must he have been through to make him like that! And he isn't old as years go— in the early thirties, I should say— but he could as easily pass for sixty. What have they done to him? What have they done to him?"

She rose quietly and walked towards him. His eyes were back on hers now, drinking in thirstily the wonder of the smile that she held on her lips. A childish eagerness came upon him, and he put out a tentative hand to touch her. Captain Foster would have restrained him, but Roxane uttered a low word. Then she put out her own hand and laid it on his arm, stroking the sleeve ever so gently while she still smiled at him. Then:

"You have been ill. You are still weak. But you are among those who will care for you and look after you. You are safe—quite safe. Do you understand? Safe! Come with me and sit down. If you wish to talk you may do so; if you wish just to rest and be quiet you may."

As one in a dream, he allowed her to lead him gently across to the low, leather chair that stood near her desk. He himself was not aware of the deep sigh that escaped him as he sank into the deep cushions. He did not know when Captain Foster and Cameron let go and drew back; he was mentally unaware when Roxane said hurriedly to Cameron:

"Please bring me a very small brandy, with just a drop of soda and angostura. He will be quite all right with me. Is he French?"

"French; but understands English well enough, ma'am—a man of some education, I should say."

"Then I shall speak to him in French. Be within call, please, captain, but leave him alone with me for a little."

The skipper seemed a little in doubt about the wisdom of this suggestion, but he would as soon have thought of questioning one of Roxane's orders as trying to jump off the bridge to the moon. He simply saluted and withdrew, but took good care to wait close at hand in the rubber-floored ante-room at the head of the companion.

When Cameron had brought the glass of spirit she had requested, he, too, was dismissed; then Roxane put the glass to her lips, took a tiny sip, and, with another wonderful smile, handed it to the poor wretch in the chair. He tried to take it, but so badly did his hand tremble that she still kept her fingers about the stem.

"Let me help," she said softly in French. "A little at a time. That is good, is it not?"

His eyes were grateful. His lips moved, and she heard him whisper:

"Merci; but, mademoiselle, are you woman or angel? Is this real?"

She laughed softly and sank into her own seat, but took good care to keep a close eye on him.

"It is very real, mon ami," she answered lightly. "You have been ill. But get it into your mind that you are now with friends. You are safe— safe. When you want to tell me how you came to be swimming in the sea so far from land—"

At the word he uttered a hoarse cry, and, shooting out a hand, clutched her with extraordinary strength, the spasm of deadly fear.

"Land! No, no, no, mademoiselle; never again take me to land!"

"Hush! You will never have to touch foot on land until you wish. No one shall harm you here."

Weak tears gushed from his eyes. In some way it seemed to filter through into his bruised, dulled mind that this was reality—that in some God-given manner he had reached a haven of safety when he had believed himself swimming into the death he sought. Blessed light streamed into his brain in that moment, and suddenly he began to talk—rapidly, incoherently, jerkily, but, nevertheless, making the rough outline of a story which Roxane could follow.

PITIFUL! It wasn't the word to describe what her ears heard in those minutes. It was the story of a crime in France, the shooting of a young wife for which he, the husband, had been held guilty, but of which he swore himself to be innocent; it was a tale of a promising career ruined—he had been a doctor, he said—by some intriguing force which he could feel but never find.

Some shred of doubt had caused the sentence to be commuted from death to penal servitude for life on Devil's Island. Ten years of that, and then for some reason, he knew not what, he had been allowed to leave the Isle of the Devil and cross to mainland at Cayenne. There he become a libere —one who must serve in the colony at forced labour time equal to that spent on Devil's Island.

A libere—a liberated one.

She knew what that meant so far as mere words could tell. Back in Marseilles Captain Foster had tried to explain; she had gathered other bits from books.

She knew of the revolting horror of the life; she had been told of the poor, half-starved, half-crazed wretches who prowled by day and night, clawing putrid scraps here and there, snatching at any bit of work that offered; of the ghastly slavery that existed when they were fanned out through the sharks of illicit labour brokers, who passed them on to blacks and half-castes for a fee; of horrors which even his twisted lips could not utter, but the tenor of which she could vaguely guess as far as her knowledge of evil would allow her to go.

Pitiful!

It was the odyssey of a soul through hell on earth to which she listened. And when he had finished, when the tears were coursing down his cheeks, she felt no shame that she found herself on her knees with her firm, white hands about his shoulders and her lips murmuring words of comfort.

She was still there when she heard a cough, and, pressing back her charge, turned to see Captain Foster standing just inside the saloon door, an expression of embarrassed apology on his face.

"I'm sorry to intrude, ma'am, but I have a report to make, and will be glad to hear your instructions."

Roxane rose but kept a detaining hand on the shoulder of the man in the chair.

"Yes, captain?"

"There is a motor-boat putting out from the coast some distance ahead, ma'am. It seems to be heading so as to cut across our bows. If it hails us shall we pay it any attention?"

"You think—"

And she made an almost imperceptible gesture towards the derelict.

The skipper nodded.

"It is as likely. There is a telephone along the coast."

Up to now the poor wretch had rested quiescent under Roxane's hand, thinking, probably, that the conversation had to do with some matter of routine of this marvellous craft into which he had been dropped. But now it mention of the coast—la cote—he began to tremble and, uttering a cry of terror, flung himself out of the chair and on to his knees, clawing at the hem of Roxane's white skirt in a frenzy.

She soothed him quickly.

"Hush! Be quiet! Have I not told you none will harm you? Have I not assured you, you are safe?"

Then she looked at the skipper.

"Bring Mr. Cameron and assist our friend to his cabin, please. Let Mr. Cameron remain with him. There will be time for you to do this and return here?"

"Yes. ma'am; Mr. Cameron is just outside."

It needed Roxane's further assurances to persuade her charge that he had nothing to fear from this new development, but at last he allowed himself to be led away. When he was gone, Roxane reseated herself at her desk and, opening the top drawer, took out a small pearl-handled revolver in a stamped leather holster that hung to a leather belt. Strapping this around her waist, she lit a fresh cigarette and sat waiting until Captain Foster returned.

"How far away, captain?"

"About half a mile now, ma'am."

"Then I shall come to the bridge with you."

"And your orders, ma'am?"

"Are we inside the three-mile limit?"

"I have already given orders to get outside the line, ma'am. We should be clear of it by now."

"Very well. We will see what this boat looks like. I will give the word whether we are to heave-to or not. If I say go ahead, see that she is driven, captain—driven to the limit."

"Ay, ay, ma'am!"

The boat, which lay almost motionless on the oily swell, was a big coastal boat fitted with a marine motor, an ugly, dirty-looking black-painted affair that held a ruffianly-looking crew of coast mongrels, and a super-ruffian in the stern. It was this individual, a fat, greasy half-caste, who was standing up in the sternsheets when Roxane reached the bridge. He was waving a white umbrella as a signal for the yacht to stop.

Roxane took a look to note that the Red Ensign was flying from the ensign staff astern, and the burgee of the Royal Canadian Yacht Club from the foremast. Then she surveyed the motor-boat load through a pair of glasses, lowered them, gave a faint shrug, and turned her back to the rail.

"We are outside the three-mile limit now, captain?"

"Yes, ma'am, well outside."

"Then there is no reason at all why we should take any notice of that collection of riff-raff. Keep right on."

And thus a very astonished half-caste was left cursing while the beautiful white yacht swept disdainfully past.

" No. 206 !" gasped the Frenchman.   "What about him ? Speak, you son of a dog !"   "He is—gone, monsieur."

MONSIEUR GASTON DUBOIS sat turning over a thick pile of flimsy yellow papers in his little office in the front of the great rambling warehouse that stood on the water-front of St. Laurent du Maroni.

It was a hot day, and although Monsieur Dubois was small and spare of frame, he seemed to feel the heat much as if he carried many more kilos of avoirdupois than he fortunately did. In one corner of the room a modern electric fan —one of the sort that swings back and forth while its blades churn the air —stirred but did not freshen the atmosphere. When it is oppressive in St. Laurent no fans made by human hands can move the damp, clinging weight of the heavy pall of air.

Yet, although the sweat was pouring down his mahogany coloured forehead and cheeks, and dripping through his close-cropped, pointed black beard —even though he wore only a pair of soiled cotton trousers and a thin, saturated cotton shirt open at the neck —Monsieur Dubois seemed equally impervious to the discomfort of the heat or of the solace of the fan. As a matter of fact, he was so immersed in running through the yellow sheets in the pile beneath his hands that he was scarcely conscious of his surroundings.

The great warehouse was silent. From the water-front came the rattle of a winch as a coasting steamer discharged a few bales of cargo which a mob of hungry liberes had pounced upon like half-famished wolves. Such pickings as these were only too rare in their miserable existence, and with a score of men to snatch at less than one well-fed man could easily handle, competition was maniacal in its ferocity.

Beyond that sign of activity, the whole water-front scorched and shimmered in the early afternoon sun. The town itself slept, from the lower quarters where the negroes and convicts herded, to the houses of the few merchants and officials on the so-called hill beyond. Only Monsieur Dubois showed energy at such an hour; and this was for the simple reason that no better time than this could be chosen for the scrutiny of those yellow papers.

Ostensibly Monsieur Dubois was an exporter of mahogany and sugar. He had a certain standing among the official French population, for he was under contract to the French Government to cut and get out as much mahogany from the limitless forests that stretched far away into the unknown as funds and the labour of the liberes would permit.

And therein lay the secret of those yellow slips.

In the French convict settlement on Devil's Island, which lies off the const of French Guiana, and is not so very far distant from the line of British Guiana, the number of serving convicts is few as compared to those classed as relegues and liberes who exist on the mainland. It has been said that the lot of a man on the island is well-nigh as terrible as is humanly conceivable; it has been written that the lot of the relegues (habitual criminals who have been turned out of the prisons in the French homeland and sent out to French Guiana to work in the forests) is infinitely worse; and it has been affirmed that, compared to these two, the existence of the poor libere (a convict who has served his sentence on the island and now must do an equal length of time on the mainland, subsisting as best he may) is an inferno.

There they are in their thousands, the relegues and the liberes— creatures, inhumanly degraded, physically and mentally, most of them, and with the soul of the damned. There they roam in that fetid, swampy forest country, trying to claw a bare subsistence out of nothing, an easy prey for any who is prepared to handle them—at the point of a gun or with the cut of a lash.

It is only natural that a widespread, illicit traffic should have grown up in the buying and selling of such creatures—a traffic that is winked at by the authorities, who know that if that were suppressed something far worse might take its place.

Yet when it comes to trading in human flesh it is only those of the stamp of Gaston Dubois who have the stomach for it. But if one can stand it—the sights, the smells, the horrors, the unspeakableness of it all—there is much money to be made. For the half-castes, petty merchants, contractors, and so on, as well as full-blooded blacks, like their labour cheap; and if it is white labour, so much the better. It is a good thing, if you have black blood in your veins, to beat the life out of one who has white blood, even if it does cost good francs to secure another to replace him when he is dead.

And each one of the yellow sheets which the convict labour broker was thumbing represented a soul sent into a deeper purgatory; meant a sum of money ranging from as low as fifty francs up to as much as five hundred. And each meant a nice profit for Gaston Dubois.

Each day did the contractor pore over the papers that showed the latest transaction entered into by his subagents; each afternoon during the hour of siesta he would total and retotal the amounts (deducting there-from the sums he had paid out in the form of commissions), so that he should be able to strike an exact balance of profit. A very nice business indeed, and one that put in Monsieur Gaston Dubois' secret bank account far fatter profits than his more open account showed from his mahogany dealings.

There were others in St. Laurent and Cayenne and other places who were engaged upon the same business, but Gaston Dubois was far and away the most important factor among them. It was he who had first choice among the eligible relegues and liberes; it was he who said "yea or "nay"; it was he whose sub-agents were dotted right along the coast and back through the forests, who kept him in close touch with the needs of new camps or the human replacements of old. The death rate is a high one.

For all his extensive organisation, it was rarely indeed that any of his agents sought him out in his office at the big water-front warehouse. There was a shack a few miles out of the town, inhabited by a pock-marked negress, which was the rendezvous when Dubois had need for personal contact with any of his men. The only one permitted to approach him at his headquarters was a wizened half-caste who had been at the game for more years than any inhabitant of St. Laurent du Maroni could remember, and who might have handled the wealth Dubois had amassed, had he possessed Dubois' brains as well as his own cunning and brutality.

But on this day when Gaston Dubois was finishing his count of the yellow slips, and when he was thinking of strolling as far as the Cercle National in order to get an iced drink, he heard the sound of a footstep on the narrow stairs.

INSTANTLY his head was up, his nostrils distended like a hound on the scent. He thought he was acquainted with every foot that mounted those steps at any hour of the day, but this, certainly, was a strange one.

With a quick movement he opened a drawer and swept the yellow slips within. In another moment he had secured an automatic pistol which he dropped into the side pocket of his coat. And, by the time a knock came at the door, he was studying a three-months-old copy of the Paris "Journal."

"Entrez!"

He called out the command without appearing to look up, but as the latch clicked and the door swung open he saw, in a carefully placed mirror opposite him, the reflection of a huge half-caste. At once he relaxed, and, jerking his head round, began to speak, softly, fluently, voicing a stream of curses.

"Imbecile!" he wound up with deceptive mildness. "Why do you not answer me? How dare you come here at this hour of the day —or at any hour?"

The bulk of the half-caste was pressed against the wall. He was in a heavy sweat, not from the heat but from fear. His glance was fearful, but it never occurred to him to protest that from the moment of his appearance he had had no chance to speak; nor that, until this moment, he had not been asked what was the reason of his coming.

"Monsieur," he faltered, "that has happened which made me think I should come to you at once. I tried to find Georges" —the wizened old devil who acted as chief agent— "but he was gone into the interior."

"So much breath wasted to say nothing! You have plenty to spare. Tell me what brings you, or I will give you cause to wish you had never seen St. Laurent at this hour of the day."

"Monsieur, pardon! I speak. It is about No. 206."

" 'Monsieur, pardon! I speak.'" mimicked the contractor dangerously. " 'It is about—'"

But there he stopped suddenly and half rose from his chair. He dropped back, his mouth working, but no words coming. At last he managed a half articulate groan. It unlocked his vocal chords.

"No. 206," he managed to gasp. "What about him? Speak, you son of a dog, or I will tear the heart out of you!"

"He is—gone, monsieur."

"Gone!"

The contractor looked as if he were going to have a seizure. His face went putty grey, his jaw muscles worked convulsively, his hands went up in the air, closing and unclosing like dirty brown talons. The half-caste started forward, but the other gestured him back. At last he conquered his rage sufficiently to speak with a sort of sinister calmness.

"You come here. You say No. 206 is gone. What do you mean? Is he dead? No, no, no; you wouldn't have said 'gone.' What has become of him? If you think you can get a plain, simple statement of fact through those thick lips of yours, please do so. If you can't I promise you I will shoot you dead where you stand! Now!"

"Monsieur, he has escaped. Have patience, I beseech you, so that I may explain. Monsieur knows that No. 206 was sent to me with special orders. I carried them out faithfully. Georges can tell you that I reported to him regularly, and he himself has visited the camp to see. He was content. He could not have lasted much longer, monsieur. His body was but a rack of bones, and his mind was going. A few more days at most, it would have been."

"Name of a dog, will you get on?" almost screamed the frantic contractor.

"Monsieur, I will proceed. It was the night before last when it was reported to me that he was missing. He could not have gone far. That was impossible. I immediately organised a search-party to scour the woods. We had the dogs as well, and with them we traced him all through the night. The trail went to the coast. How he managed to reach it, how he could cover the distance of sixteen kilometres or more, I do not know, monsieur. But he did so, and when we got there we came upon a negro who informed us that one answering to the description, one who looked like a relegue or a libere, had taken to the water and begun to swim out to sea."

He paused then and shook his great head as if, even now, he could not credit that such a thing could be. But the murderous look in the contractor's eyes brought him back to his tale.

"I at once took steps, monsieur. We had at hand no boat, but as it was just on the point of dawn it was possible to make our way along by the beach to the fishing village of St. Brine. There was trouble about the boat, monsieur, but I managed it, and by the time we were ready to put to sea in search of his body—for I knew monsieur would want proof—or to make sure that he had become sharks' meat, a negro came in to report that he had been watching a man swim far out from the shore, and, while swimming, had been picked up by a white ship that was passing.

"Monsieur, I swear to you by the saints, that I looked up then, and, out at sea, just as the black had said, was such a white ship, a beautiful ship, monsieur. So what did I do? I launched the boat at once, monsieur, and put out to head off the ship and collect our property.

"We reached her in good time, and, standing up in the stem, I waved my umbrella to attract attention."

GASTON DUBOIS lifted his hand for silence. Slowly he got up from his chair, the act revealing how small was his stature compared to that of the huge man by the door. Walking across to a cupboard, he opened it and took out a bottle of old cognac. He poured himself a stiff dose of the potent spirit and drank it off neat. Then he closed and locked the cupboard, and, turning, showed his teeth in an extraordinary mirthless grin.

"So you saw the beautiful white ship, did you?" he asked softly. "And, not satisfied with allowing a man who was already dead to escape —a dead man who could travel sixteen kilometres at night through the forest and swamps —ha, ha! —you went out in a boat and stood up and waved your umbrella! And what else did you do, my good gros Jean?"

"Why, why, monsieur, they took no notice!"

"Did you expect them to stop and invite you on board? Did you think they would make special dejeuner for you? Were you disappointed that you were not asked to sit beneath the awning and drink an iced aperitif? You saw so much, my good gros Jean, did you see anything on your way here?"

"Why, yes, monsieur. I saw the same ship in harbour."

"Hah! Splendid! He saw the same ship in harbour! And do you know who came in that ship, my good gros Jean? You don't? I will tell you, then. A very rich lady came in her —a lady with letters to the governor of the colony. Do you understand that? And you, with your crazy old umbrella, would stop such a ship at sea and ask if, by any chance, they happened to have a stray libere on board!"

The big man by the door shivered, he knew that Gaston Dubois was never more dangerous than when he was in this soft, mocking mood. There were tales whispered of things that had happened at the camps back in the depths of the forest that made one turn and look behind one when the sun sank and darkness plunged down between the trees.

But, for the time being, the contractor seemed to have forgotten the other. Dropping into the chair at his desk, he put his head in his hands and gave himself up to thought.

No more serious report than this could have been brought to him. No. 206 was something very special in the way of liberes; or, at least, one might think so, to judge from the heavy fee which Gaston Dubois had received, together with an anonymous letter giving him explicit instructions us to what was to be done with the fellow.

Just what lay behind it all he could not guess. Some intrigue in very high circles in France, he imagined. What he did know was that No. 206 had been convicted of wife murder in France, had been sentenced to the guillotine, had had his sentence commuted to one of life imprisonment on Devil's Island, had been released from the island at the end of ten years, and had landed on the mainland as a libere.

Almost immediately the heavy fee with the letter had reached Gaston Dubois. He had acted at once. He would have handled a hundred liberes for that price. He was requested to see that No. 206 should be sent to the worst possible camp among the relegues; that he should be killed gradually by privation but not by actual physical means; that he should on no account be allowed to escape.

And now he was gone! Was this half-caste imbecile speaking the truth when he said the fugitive had been picked up at sea by the white yacht that had come into harbour the evening before? Was it possible for a man in his mental and physical condition to stumble through sixteen kilometres of forest and swamp during one night without food or any form of nourishment, and then take to the sea and swim through shark-infested water for several more kilometres? If so, could pigs fly?

On the other hand, suppose it were true? If he were on board that yacht, what account had he given of himself? Certainly those on the yacht had made no mention of any such incident since their arrival in port.

Then what lay behind it all? Just what sort of a pawn in what sort of big game was No. 206? And was that cool beauty of a russet-haired girl who brought letters to the governor mixed up in it? Was that escape and the picking up a planned affair? If so, who had helped No. 206 to make his getaway?

There was something behind it all that put a chill of acute uneasiness upon the heart of Gaston Dubois; and, realising that he might be treading on very dangerous ground, he decided that the best thing to do immediately was to send the half-caste back to his camp. He would speak more gently to him, in case he should get panic-stricken and open his mouth too wide.

"All right, my good gros Jean," he said quietly, lifting his head.

"I am sure you did your best. Get back to your camp now, but on the way see that word is sent to Georges to come here at once. In the meantime, I will take measures to find out if the fellow is on board that white yacht."

"It won't be necessary to go to any trouble, Monsieur Dubois," came a light, cool, slightly husky voice from the gloom of the hall just outside the door. "I am here to give you any information you may wish—and to extract some."

The half-caste sprang to one side as if he had been pricked with a steel brad. As for Gaston Dubois, he sat paralysed, gazing upon such a vision of feminine loveliness as never before had illumined that abode of crooked intent.

Chapter 4.   In the Forest.

NO body of men have been more congenial or more imbued with the spirit of camaraderie and esprit de corps than the little company that made up the personnel of the Franco-British Guiana Expedition.

Eight Europeans there were in all, and each man a specialist. In compliment to the country in whose territory they were operating, a Frenchman had been appointed to the command— Colonel Marcel Forres, Chevalier of the Legion of Honour and lecturer at the Sorbonne on the Ethnology of South American races.

Second in command was Professor William Ferguson, of the London Institute of Tropical Diseases; and, in the general company, Mr. Sexton Blake, of London, who was carrying out research work in connection with the manufacture of obscure poisons by the natives from a bewildering variety of plants, herbs, and animal matter; Professor Gregory —British —and Professor Colbert —French—who were working jointly in a preliminary classification of the trees and larger shrubs of the Guiana forests; a geologist; a mineralogist and a pestologist, who worked partly in conjunction with Professor Ferguson, and, at times, with Sexton Blake. Eight men, who, even in the few weeks since they had gone inland from Cayenne, had been through sufficient hardships to test the mettle of each, and to find therein something for mutual respect.

The permanent camp was pitched in a small glade close to the Cunimarca River, and immediately above the beautiful falls of the same name. Further in the depths of the forest of giant trees— mahogany, lignum vitae, and many three hundred-foot "saplings" yet to be identified— was one subsidiary camp; half a mile higher up the Cunimarca was a second subsidiary post, used mostly by Sexton Blake, Gifford, the mineralogist, Parsons, the geologist, and young Field, the pestologist.

The permanent staff of camp workers, tree climbers, and specimen collectors consisted of a dozen or so scrubs, relegues and liberes, picked up in Cayenne, with between twenty and thirty —the number always varying— Escumarca Indians, the latter being used entirely for work in the forest and along the stream.

The relegues and liberes were a hard-bitten, murderous, thieving, unreliable lot, who needed watching night and day, and who would have cleaned out the camp at the slightest sign of weakness on the part of those in authority. They might even have accomplished something of the sort in any case, were it not for the ceaseless vigil kept over them by two heavily-armed guards— one a gigantic ex-British soldier, whom Sexton Blake had picked up in Demerara on the way down the coast, and who had had previous experience in all the Guianas; the other a French sailor, who had "outed" the mate of his own ship and taken to the jungle.

Not a very desirable outfit in many ways, but mixed, as is necessarily the case on an expedition of that sort in a country that is only civilised on the fringe —if civilisation can be claimed for the appalling conditions that exist in that steaming hades into which the worst criminals of France are poured.

Yet the little body of scientists went on with their work as cheerfully and imperturbably as if they were following the ordinary tame routine in Paris or London. Of the actual work being performed, the most spectacular, and certainly the most picturesque, was the forestry.

From the ground one craned one's neck to see the giants towering high above, straight as arrows and ending in wide-spreading vaulted arches of greenery, which one might think to be the ceiling of some vast cathedral.

But when ropes were slung through the topmost branches, by means of thin lines sent up first by the Indian tree climbers, and a swinging cradle hauled up, from which one could make a closer study of the foliage, one saw, still higher, a second roof, where the most hoary old patriarchs looked down disdainfully upon the upstart saplings beneath.

And, too, from the cathedral aisles beneath, one saw only grey forms flitting through the occasional patches where dappled sunlight showed, or heard the harsh screech of parrot, paraket, and macaw; but from the vantage point of an observation chair one could watch an extraordinary display of vivid colours, where the sun threw every feather into wonderful gloss.

But just as useful was the stone-hammering of the mineralogist or the geologist, the dissection of insects by the pestologist, the slow classifications of the botanist; and, not least of any of these, the dangerous experimental work among obscure poisons which Sexton Blake, the famous private detective, of London, was carrying out.

Apart from what he hoped to contribute to the general results of the expedition—and he had felt distinctly honoured at being invited to join this distinguished band of scientists—the famous criminologist expected to gather important material for an appendix to the well-known and authoritative monograph on rare poisons which he had published some time previously. Hence the ruthless way in which he had wound up all current cases of major importance in London and left those of minor routine in the hands of his capable young assistant, Tinker, in order not to loose the opportunity.

For the first ten days or so all the activities had been preliminary, so to say —the choosing of the camp sites, the unpacking of instruments, kit, scientific paraphernalia, and the organising of the work to be done. Then the actual breaking of ground, each man in his own special direction, and the gradual settling down to the routine that they hoped would last for a matter of seven or eight weeks — unless the seasonal rains drove them out before.

Riding the subject in which he was so keenly interested, Blake had little or no thought for criminal matters in particular. His attention was solely concerned with them in the abstract, and, certainly, he would have been the last one to admit the possibility of anything touching on the criminally mysterious interfering with his present occupation. So does man little know of the kick which Fate is holding in waiting to administer at the least expected moment.

THE first sign of any such thing came in an evening when, in company with Field, the young pestologist. Blake tramped along by the edge of the Cunimarca to the main camp.

It had been a good day's work; he was pleased with results, and particularly interested in the coagulating properties of sap exuded by a somewhat rare plant which Professor Gregory had sent along to him. There was a hope in Blake's mind that this quick-hardening sap might be the base of one of the Mayan Indian poisons of which he was trying to find the secret, and he was talking of this to his companion when they swung into sight of the glade.

In the forest close at hand day was already gone. On the bank of the stream there was still a patch of light to be seen, a canyon cutting between the dense growth that reached almost to the sheer edge of each bank and almost touched overhead. In the glade it was just at the half-light when darkness may engulf one at any moment, and they could see that the petrol camp lantern had already been lighted.

Their first view showed several men in thin, tropical khaki, standing near to where two of the lanterns hung, all seemingly absorbed in what was being said by another man, who stood in front of them.

This latter individual Blake recognised as Pilcher, the expedition foreman he had picked up in Demerara. The attitude of the group and that of the man told them that something was wrong, and Blake said as much to Field as he quickened his steps.

"It looks like it. Blake, wonder what's up?"

"Some trouble with the men. I expect. I've noticed a sort of restlessness among the liberes and relegues ever since the night before last. Did anything strike you?"

"Not particularly, except that I did hear two of them speak in an insolent way to Martin."

"I don't see him there with Pilcher."

By this time they were almost across the glade and, at sight of them, the group turned their eyes towards them. Pilcher, who had been speaking —and who, despite the fact that Blake was not the leader of the expedition seemed to look to him for orders —broke off what he was saying. Professor Ferguson was in the centre of the party, a big, virile man who was totally unlike the popular conception of a pedant. He hailed Blake in a bull-like voice that had made the rafters of many a lecture-room ring to the echo.

"What do you think of this, Blake? Pilcher says every mongrel libere and relegue, has cleared out and taken a good slice of our stuff along. It must have been well prearranged, for they managed it in less than ten minutes, just before they were to draw their evening rations."

Blake realised the seriousness of the news. It had not been an easy job to get reliable men together to come into the jungle, even though work with the expedition offered better pay, better food, and infinitely better living conditions than slavery under some forest sub-contractor getting out mahogany.

They had been forced to take what offered, but there had been no lack of volunteers of the class. Their difficulty had been to drive off those whom they could not put on the pay roll. Therefore it was distinctly puzzling to understand why they had deserted in a body. Concerted and carefully prearranged action it must have been, as suggested by Professor Ferguson.

Blake glanced at Pilcher.

"Did Pilcher see them go?" he asked, directing his question at the professor.

"No, Mr. Blake. Martin was in charge at the time and I was over at the cook tent seeing about the rations. When I came out I couldn't see anyone but the few Indians who were on duty in camp. I thought Martin must be marching them round another way, but soon found I was wrong."

"And Martin? Why didn't he hold them?"

Pilcher rubbed his hand against one thigh and hesitated.

"Pilcher isn't keen on casting suspicion on Martin, Blake," broke in Professor Ferguson. "But it seems that Martin went with them, though whether willingly or by force we do not know."

"Well, chief, Field tells me he heard two of them speak insolently to Martin, so perhaps he went unwillingly."

"That is possible. What I can't understand is their motive, Blake. Neither can any of the others. Martin was armed. It was his job to hold them. But he apparently didn't make a sound. Unless he went willingly, then they must have rushed him without warning. What worries me is the stuff they took with them?"

"Is it serious?"

"A lot of food; that doesn't matter. But they have a couple of rifles, several hundred rounds of ammunition and, worst of all, our largest medicine chest."

"Will you go in pursuit?"

"That is just what we were debating when you came up. We are all in favour of trying to recover the medicine chest and rifles and ammunition. It doesn't matter about the food; we can send a messenger into Cayenne and get another lot of bearers to bring out more.

"Pilcher says you can do more with the Indians than anyone else, and as we should need them if we start a chase, we thought it best that you have a palaver with their headman. They may know a lot about the affair."

"Very good, professor, I'll see what I can get out of him."

SLIPPING a canvas rucksack from his shoulders, Blake strode out of the glare of the lanterns and crossed towards the camp-fire where the Escumarcas were gathered round a huge steaming pot. Others of the Indians were just straggling in from the two subsidiary camps, but the headman, whose dignity would not permit of his doing anything in the form of actual work, was seated on an Arawakan blanket smoking and dividing his glances between his men in one direction and the cooking-pot in another.

He rose with dignified leisure as Blake made a sign to him. Two other members of the party spoke his tongue after a fashion, but this lean white man not only knew it fluently, but could converse with him about his own country that lay many leagues up tortuous streams in the valley of the Essequibo —could talk in a knowing way of the secret poisons of the different tribes, of the little-known method of shrinking a human head until it was no larger than an orange, and of the legendary white races that had built mysterious cities far in the interior many, many moons before.

He made a gesture of respectful attention and waited.

Blake regarded him in silence for a few minutes. There was no telling just how much smattering of the argot of the country the old chief and his men might possess. For years they had been in touch with the white men, trading balata, gold, semi-precious stones and various tribal products for cloths, blankets, guns, ammunition and so on. It stood to reason they must have picked up sufficient of the lingua franca of the coast for the purposes of trade and, knowing them as a deep, reserved people, Blake was inclined to think they might have overheard quite a lot if the deserters had carried on their plotting within hearing.

But they would say nothing, out of fear or because it was none of their business what happened between the white men and the ex-convicts, upon whom they looked with supreme contempt.

"There will be plenty of food to-night for your men, Great Chief of the Escumarcas," said Blake at last.

"Their bellies have been well-filled, brother," admitted the Indian. "The white brothers do not give with one hand and take with the other."

"You are satisfied, then, Great Chief?"

"In plenty, brother."

"Is it because their bellies were empty that the others have gone away, red brother?"

Eyes of Indian met eyes of white man, and one pair could not have been more non-committal than the other. Yet in that gaze there was mutual respect and liking.

"Is it then that the white brothers did not send away those who have departed?"

"Is it not known differently to you, red brother? It is not in our minds to feel sorrow at their going. They were lazy dogs. But they have stolen that of great value, and thou, Great Chief, know well that we put no guard on those things which we value. While the Escumarcas were here we felt safe. And one who acted as guard is gone with them.

"I come to you, red brother, to aid me. Shall it be that we go in search of them? Or is there much trickery behind? Have they spoken with the forked tongue?"

The chief did not respond to Blake, but, turning, spoke in a rapid, guttural language to a young Indian, who was engaged in plaiting a grass rope, the lingo being one that Blake had never heard before. The young brave leaped to his feet and pointed towards a certain point in the belt of trees, that now looked like a dense purple wall surrounding them, cutting them off entirely from the outside world. He said a few words —not more than half a dozen in all; then he resumed his task.

The headman turned back to Blake. "If the white brother will come alone I will show. Then he may read."

"Before the time of food?"

"I am ready."

"Wait for me, red brother."

With that, Blake hastened back to where the others were waiting.

"There is something up, all right, professor. The headman knows what has been going on, but won't speak yet. He has something to show me in the forest. I think I had better go with him."

"Then two or three of us will accompany you, Blake."

"He insists that I shall go alone. I shall be all right. I believe I can trust him. There are certain reasons; I shall take a weapon, and will not go too far. If I need help I will shoot three times in rapid succession."

At that moment Colonel Forres, the technical leader, though he was too engrossed in the scientific side of matters to pay much attention to the material phase—preferring to leave that end of it to the virile and indefatigable Professor Ferguson—came out of his tent to inquire what was wrong. When matters had been explained he expressed strong disapproval of Blake's suggestion, but at this point Professor Ferguson endorsed Blake's side of it, and, as usual, the little Frenchman yielded. As a matter of fact, he trotted back into his tent almost immediately after, and it was safe betting that within three minutes he had forgotten all about the matter.

Blake saw to his automatic, and strapped on Field's weapon as a spare.

Then he rejoined the headman, and, with the latter in the lead, started for the point in the forest ring to which the young Indian had pointed. He held up his electric torch just before they plunged into a narrow path, and, seeing that his companion made no gesture of disapproval, switched it on.

The Indian travelled with such directness of purpose and speed that Blake could almost have believed he was revisiting a spot he knew well; but, knowing the Escumarcas as he did, he was quite satisfied the old man was simply following the brief, but, for him, ample directions given by the young brave.

Twisting in and out, they covered what Blake estimated to be some three hundred yards or so. Then suddenly the headman stopped and drew to one side, pointing. Blake swung the torch up so it rested on an object that hung from the lower branch of a young sapling. It was not a pretty sight to look at, but his duty drove him closer. And then he found the answer to the mystery of Martin's disappearance.

They had finished him off in brutal mutilation before hauling him up by the wrists and pinning a piece of dirty paper to the front of his khaki tunic. It read:

"Beware. We go, but we return. The day of the liberes and the relegues is come."

The headman drew to one side and stopped. Blake swung the torch up so that it played on the man who hung by the wrists.

Chapter 5.   *Danger Ahead.*

OVER the evening meal the little band of Europeans discussed the revolting and puzzling discovery Blake had made.

For some reason which even Blake could not elicit, none of the Indians would touch the corpse of the ex-sailor. It may have been some superstition regarding his manner of death, or it may have been in fear of those who had done the murder. They would never reveal the truth; nor would the headman urge them on.

Thus it was left to Blake, with the assistance of Field, Clifford, and Pilcher to bring what was left of the poor wretch back to camp. There, late that night, they buried him, with a giant mahogany tree as a headstone.

But first they must discuss this strange development. Colonel Forres managed to drag his mind from the scientific problems that were besotting him sufficiently to take a listening interest; the others threshed the thing out in every possible way. But always they came back to the same point which Sexton Blake had advanced at the very beginning.

"I can understand a treacherous, criminal lot like the liberes and relegues clearing out from the conditions that are usually theirs in this country," remarked the detective. "Nor could one blame them, for we all know what a ghastly existence it is. But what puzzles me is why they should leave us.

"What they took with them doesn't amount to sufficient to reward such a number for desertion. A couple of guns, some ammunition, a bit of tinned food, and the medicine chest. It isn't enough. Besides, there are a good many leagues of tough jungle for them to negotiate before they reach the most primitive form of civilisation where they could renew their supplies. But even granting all that; let us say that the more domineering element among them were just plain fed-up, and wanted to get back where they could drink freely; let us agree that they fixed it among them to decamp at such and such an hour on such and such a day, and chose that hour when Pilcher would be in the cook-tent and Martin on guard, because they knew they could handle Martin more easily than Pilcher. If all that is so, why didn't they turn Martin loose later on?

"They would be well away by that time, and practically out of danger of any pursuit we might organise. But they didn't do that.

They only waited until they were some three hundred yards away from the camp, almost within earshot of any of us who happened to be about; in view, I should say, of some of the Indians who were straggling back at that hour. They murdered him in most brutal fashion.

"There was viciousness in the way it was done; there was degenerate cruelty, but there was also a bravado that is deeply puzzling. And what was even more insolent bravado, was the message they had pinned on to the murdered man's tunic. Mark my words, gentlemen, there is something behind that action —something sinister, something they know about of which we are, so far, in ignorance."

"I agree with Mousieur Blake," remarked Colonel Forres, nodding his shaggy head. "The message is the keynote. Do you not agree, mon cher Ferguson?"

The big professor was smoking a huge pipe and gazing through the clouds of smoke towards the rampart of the near-by forest. He inclined his head in agreement, but did not speak. Professors Gregory and Colbert made an assenting gesture, and it was a foregone conclusion that Parsons, Clifford, and Field were with Blake to a man.

At last Professor Ferguson spoke.

"I've been thinking along lines that are expressed in your last words, Blake. You say, 'something they knew about, of which we are, so far, in ignorance.' Well, I agree with you. But what can it be?

"What can be going on outside the range of our camp that should be of such far-reaching effect as to affect those treacherous ex-convicts and yet of which we couldn't get even a whisper? There can't be anything really widespread happening in the country. If that wireless of ours hadn't gone phut two nights ago we might be getting some news through."

"I'm not sure, now, that it wasn't put out of order with deliberate intent," remarked Blake. "It is curious that our one direct link with the outside should be destroyed on the same night that I detected insolence of manner on the part of two of the liberes in speaking to Martin."

"What about our bearer?" put in Gregory. "Shouldn't he have arrived back from Cayenne to-night?"

Several pairs of eyes narrowed suddenly.

"That's right!" came from man after man. "I'd forgotten about the bearer. He may bring news, if there is any, that will explain the defection."

"If he gets through," said Blake quietly. "We know what happened to Martin. Martin was murdered because it was intended that he should not be able to tell us anything. The bearer may be killed for the same reason, if they meet him. Gentlemen, I can't get it out of my head that there is something very queer underneath all this. I think—"

HIS remark was interrupted by a short, challenging call in a voice they recognised at Pilcher's. The big foreman had been prowling about uneasily between the cook tent and the general camp-fire for some time, and had, apparently, seen or heard something to rouse his suspicions. As one man they came to their feet and stood looking. By the ruddy flames of the big fire they saw the shadowy bulk of his form blend with the heavy wall of the forest. Then they heard his voice again in a low growl of what sounded like relief; next moment he reappeared with a small figure beside him.

"The bearer!"

It was Field who spoke, but the others only nodded, watching while Pilcher brought his companion across the open ground.

But Field was right. The bearer had got through. It was the Indian runner who was sent into St. Laurent once a week for letters and light necessaries which could be carried in his pack.

Even before he reached them they could see that he walked as one on the verge of dropping, but there was nothing very remarkable in that, since the Escumarca runners would cover an enormous distance in a day and keep it up for a week on end on scarcely any sustenance beyond mate leaves. Most of them had seen a runner stagger into camp in just such condition as this, and be as fresh as paint by the following morning.

There was something in the man's manner, however, that told them he was suffering from no ordinary fatigue. But they did not see the reason until, after a respectful salute, he dropped to his knees and slid his pack to the ground.

Then, in the flesh of the back, just where the lower edge of the pack had rested, they could see a great wound that had formed a long, wide crust after profuse bleeding. How the stoical endurance of even an Indian could endure with flesh and ligaments and muscles ripped in such terrible fashion was a mystery.

Blake and Professor Ferguson were the first to spring forward and catch him, and, speaking in the man's own tongue, Blake chided him.

"With this wound you should have left the bag," he said kindly. "You must have it attended to at once and then take a long rest. After, you can tell us how it happened."

The man shook his head.

"The Great Chief will heal it, brother. It is a scratch such as the Escumarca heeds not. The bag must be brought, for the Escumarca is one of his promise. But before I go to the Great Chief, it is written that I must tell the white brothers of what I have seen."

"It can wait," Blake reassured him.

"It must be heard, brother. There are men of evil in among the great trees. They came upon me unawares and shot at me. They were the same who were the white brothers' slave-men. They carry the sticks that kill without throwing. But Stream Runner was more fleet of foot and left them behind."

Blake shot a significant glance at Professor Ferguson.

"What we feared! This man is a good deal of a hero, professor."

Then to the Indian: "Just another word, Stream Runner. You have proved yourself a valiant Escumarca this day, and your reward will be great. Were these men of evil coming towards the camp?"

"No, brother, they were seeking the path that would take them to Mantaca" (the Escumarca name for St. Laurent.).

"And thought they would cut him off before he could reach us." said Blake. "Well, perhaps they will think even now that he could not make it."

He laid a hand on the Indian's shoulder.

"Will you not let the Great White Chief look to your back?"

"No, brother! The Great Chief yonder knows that which will heal his children most quickly."

Blake knew that he would be unhappy if anyone but the headman were allowed to touch the wound, so he did not press the point signing to Pilcher to take him across to the fire, he turned to Colonel Forres and Professor Ferguson as the two leaders.

"There is something afoot, gentlemen. Perhaps our letters will enlighten us. If not, or, perhaps, in any event, I have a suggestion to make."

"Let us get through the letters, then, messieurs."

It was the leader who spoke, and Field, as the youngest, plunged into the bag to take out a packet of blood-soaked letters which had helped to save the Indian's life when the bullet ripped through the canvas.

THE one item brought to light that gave even a slight hint as to what might be wrong, was a letter to Colonel Forres from the Commandant of St. Laurent. It was an official document, which, after touching on one or two matters that had no bearing on the subject in question, went on:

I am uncertain, my dear Colonel, whether to insist that you curtail your expedition and return at once to St. Laurent or Cayenne. If I do so I expect you will appeal to the Governor at Cayenne and my orders will be ignored. I am somewhat uneasy, nevertheless, at the way things are going at present.

For some reason which, so far, is a mystery, the liberes and relegues are showing signs of great unrest. You know those specimens, my dear Colonel, and with many thousands of them in the country there are always possibilities for mischief, dogs and sweepings that they are.

I have plenty of troops in hand to take care of St. Laurent, but if a sudden crisis occurred I could not guarantee the safety of any white persons outside this radius. The care of the Cayenne district is, of course, in the hands of his Excellency, whom I have already advised of the turn things have taken here. He telegraphs me that he sees very few signs of similar unrest in his district.

Of course, neither the liberes nor the relegues have any arms or ammunition that we know of, but they possess knives and machetes, and we know what damage can be done with those weapons.

My latest news is that most of the Government contractors have lost complete control of their gangs, and that in many cases mobs have taken to wandering among the woods, raiding small native and half-caste villages. Indeed, several hundreds have drifted into St. Laurent; but I shall make short shrift of those.

There is, too, an almost complete suspension of business among the unofficial labour contractors. I am wondering if some Communist agitators have got into the country without our knowledge and have been spreading dangerous propaganda. It may be that you will feel no effects of the unrest in your far camp, but I write you in warning, and if you receive an order from me to strike camp and return at once to

Cayenne or St. Laurent I shall expect you to regard it as an order that must be obeyed; also I am concerned for the British subjects who are with your party.

That was the tenor of the letter written three days before. What events had taken place since then they could not guess. But they did know what had happened in their own small sphere, and, to use the commandant's words, it would not have appeared likely that they would be affected in their distant camp. But they had felt it already, to the extent of the murder of Martin and the decamping of every libere and relegue on the job

"Which means," remarked Colonel Forres thoughtfully— "which means, messieurs, that in some way unknown to us, someone has crept up through the forest and whispered mischief into the ears of those wretches who were in our employ."

"There can be no doubt of that, sir," agreed Blake. "And for just that reason, mon colonel, I beg you to grant me permission to start at once for St. Laurent."

"Mais! What is this, Monsieur Blake? Are you mad? Start for St. Laurent? For what purpose, tell me if you please —to receive a bullet from ambush? To have your throat cut while you sleep?"

"No, sir. I pray you to listen for a moment. We must have more food supplies soon. It is true we can live off the country for a certain length of time if driven to it, but there is danger in that. Moreover, we are perilously short of medicines; we shall need fresh camp hands, for the Escumarcas will not do this work. And we ought to know just how things are going. It may be that I can pick up a dozen dependable men who could assist us to defend the camp if necessary. I am taking it for granted, sir, that you will not strike camp at this stage."

The noted French savant nearly exploded at Blake's last words.

"Strike camp!" he stuttered. "Clear out for a lot of mangy not-to-be-mentioned sons of dogs! Sir, I commanded during the War —but I grow excited, my dear Blake. Let us discuss the thing 'round-table' as you say. Come, messieurs, you have heard the suggestions: What is the vote?"

Boiled down, the vote consisted of almost every man volunteering to go as well. But to each and all Blake shook his head.

"Let me take one Indian, that is all." he urged. "I needn't go by the trail. We can find a canoe —leave that to the Indian —and get down by way of the Cunamarca and the Manataca into the lagoon and reach St. Laurent in two days and a half as against our nine days coming in. It will be quicker than making for Cayenne. I know the lingo, and I can make better time by travelling light. If you insist, then let, say, Professor Colbert, come with me, so there will be one of your race, Colonel Forres, with me."

It was argued down and down until the rock-bottom base Blake had set was reached. And there the consent was given. Within half an hour of permission he and Professor Colbert were ready, taking for arms an automatic pistol each and one rifle in Blake's care. For guide they had the young Indian who had pointed out to the headman where he should seek to read the mystery of Martin's disappearance.

The little man rolled over and over, even after hitting the pavement, and fetched up against Blake's leg. Before he could scramble to his feet the sailor was upon him.

Chapter 6.   Money to Burn.

WHILE the tropic dawn was still fresh two dilapidated figures turned out of the Rue de Grasse in St. Laurent on to the wide stretch of the water-front.

It would have been difficult for anyone who had seen a party of sprucely-clad European scientists leave Cayenne some three weeks before, to recognise the pair as forming part of the personnel of that group.

Both were unshaven and worse than unkempt. Their khaki garments were torn and stained with every variety of mud afforded by the jungle; one of them limped stiffly; the other carried his left arm in an improvised sling. The elder was without a hat; that of his companion was a travesty of the bit of headgear it had been some days previously.

To add to their uninviting appearance, which made them almost ferociously repelling, each had a heavy automatic pistol strapped prominently round his waist, while one carried a rifle in the hollow of his arm.

Twice since entering the town they had been stopped and questioned by guards, but on each occasion the elder of the two had spoken curt words which had passed them on their way.

Two nights before they had started from the base camp of the Franco-British Guiana Expedition, and their journey to St. Laurent had been made in record time. Once they had had a nasty brush with a gang of liberes and relegues whom they had encountered, but their fire had proved too hot for the ex-convicts, though they had not passed the ambush without being marked. In a small hut outside the town lay the Indian who had guided them through, a deep knife-wound in his side.

Thus the arrival of Sexton Blake and Professor Colbert of the Paris Sorbonne at the jumping-off place for Devil's Island. At the moment of turning into the water-front their intention was to reach by the shortest way a small hotel where they knew they would be able to get what attention they needed before calling on the commandant of the port, Colonel Lucien Favre.

It would hardly be in keeping, despite their standing, to appear at his residence looking like two scarecrows. But scarcely had they passed the corner than the taller of the two drew up with a muttered exclamation and, grasping his companion by his unwounded arm, brought him to a halt.

"What is it, mon ami?"

Sexton Blake was gazing out into the harbour where a beautiful white yacht lay serenely at anchor. Scarcely more than a biscuit toss away she loomed, large and noticeable in comparison with the dingy little craft that kept her company. And her stern that lay towards them bore the name and port of registration that could easily be read at the distance—La Brise, Montreal. In further confirmation of her origin the burgee of the Royal Canadian Yacht Club hung at her mast.

Sexton Blake did not answer at once, but urged Professor Colbert back round the corner. Only when they were out of sight of the yacht did he pause.

"The matter is that yacht, Colbert," he said rapidly. "What the devil is she doing here in St. Laurent?"

The Frenchman shrugged, then glanced at Blake keenly, thinking his friend was suffering from a touch of fever after the malaria-infested streams and swamps they had negotiated.

"What should she be doing here, Blake? A rare bird to enter this harbour, I grant you, but probably the private yacht of some rich person who is cruising this coast. Let it not worry you, mon ami. We shall soon be at the hotel."

Blake laughed suddenly.

"Don't think I have suddenly gone light in the head, Colbert. Of course you do not understand. But it struck me as odd, decidedly odd, to see that particular craft lying there just now."

"Tiens! Then you know her?"

"I should say I do; and the owner, if it is still the same."

"Then perhaps we can find hospitality there instead of at the hotel," responded the Frenchman naively. "It would be nice to have a real bath again, and she looked as if she would be well provided that way."

"She is, Colbert, she is; hot freshwater baths, hot salt-water baths, electric baths, needle baths[1]—anything you want. And iced drinks my friend! But it is the very last place we shall go at present. But I will explain later. Let us go on. There is no reason why we should not pass her."

---

[1] An electric bath is a tanning bed; a needle bath is a shower.

More puzzled than ever at Blake's sudden change of purpose, the Frenchman gave the inevitable shrug and told himself that he was right, that Blake really did have a touch of fever. He allowed Blake to haul him round the corner again, but for the second time the detective came to a stop at the sight that met their eyes.

JUST coming away from the side of the yacht was a small white boat manned by half a dozen sailors in snowy uniforms, who pulled in beautiful rhythm. But that was the least arresting part of the picture.

In the sternsheets, a vision in white, was a girl with a silk parasol shading her face from the horizontal rays of the sun that still lay low in the east. Sensing that something about her had brought his companion's feet to this second pause, the Frenchman showed less signs of irritation. Like all his race, he was susceptible to a pretty woman, and he had seen nothing like this vision since leaving France.

"What is it, mon ami? Surely you are not afraid of a pretty woman? It is meat and drink after what we have been through."

"Maybe," was the non-committal answer. "We'll wait nevertheless, Colbert. In any case, you could not have her inspect you in those rags."

"Tiens! I had forgotten what scarecrows we are. You are right. We will wait. But who is she?"

"She is the owner. I'll tell you all about her later. I wonder where she is bound at this early hour."

As if in answer to his query, a pair of white mules came racing out of a side street on to the water-front, drawing after them an open landau such as was a rare sight in a place like St. Laurent. On the box was a negro driver in Government uniform and, beside him, another negro similarly garbed. Both Blake and Colbert needed no more than this to tell them the carriage could only belong to the commandant, Colonel Lucien Favre.

It swung round recklessly, drew up at the sheer edge of the quay, and the footman was on the ground with the door open by the time the girl in white tripped lightly up the steps from the landing-stage. As if it were a matter of regular routine, she stepped into the landau, which immediately set off with a clutter along the cobbled way, with a dozen yelping curs after it.

Colbert made some remark apropos it being the commandant's carriage, but Blake was in deep thought and made no answer.

It should mean nothing to him that the yacht La Brise should be lying at anchor at such an out-of-the-way place as St. Laurent du Maroni, in French Guiana. Nor should it mean any more to him that the fair owner, Roxane Harfield, should have flashed across his ken in the same place. She was the owner of the yacht with, apparently, unlimited means at her disposal, and was entitled to cruise where she would.

But, somehow, Blake could not get out of his mind what had led up to his first (and, until now, last) meeting with her. He remembered what she had said on that occasion; he recalled only too vividly the vow she had expressed —that she would never rest until she had brought to book the eight men who had swindled her father back in Canada and, through this had caused her mother's death from shock.

Was she, then, still pursuing her purpose? he was asking himself. If so, was it this aim that had brought her to St. Laurent? In that case, which one of those eight men could she expect to find here? He knew that her first victim, Harold Carruthers, the Montreal stockbroker, had been disposed of, and he had to concede her a certain success in that direction, even if he had got back from her the sixty thousand pounds which she had taken from Carruthers.

But there were seven others in that group, or would be if they were all alive. It was quite possible they had scattered about the globe, but what would bring one of them to such a place as French Guiana unless us a convict?

With his limp they were making slow progress along the front when they saw two of the sailors from the yacht's boat appear at the top of the steps by the landing jetty and roll across towards the footpath that they were following. Some little distance still separated them when the two sailors disappeared from view beneath a sign that proclaimed the premises as the Cafe Napoleon.

The chance of a meeting had not caused Blake to seek to avoid recognition. He knew it was quite probable that the pair had been part of the personnel of La Brise when he and Tinker were prisoners on board, but there was little chance of their recognising him in brief passing in his present dilapidated condition.

On the other hand, he had already made up his mind that it didn't matter. There was no reason why he should endeavour to conceal his presence in St. Laurent from Roxane Harfield. On the contrary, the more he considered the matter the more inclined he was to seek a meeting, for he was not a little curious to know what lay behind her visit to the port.

His thoughts were brought back to their immediate surroundings by the sound of a commotion a little way ahead, and, as it grew louder, they knew it came from the Cafe Napoleon. Voices were raised in heated altercation, one high-pitched and hysterical in tone, two others deep and blasphemous; all were speaking English.

Blake and Colbert were almost opposite the entrance when the affair, whatever it was, reached a crisis. Out of the doorway shot a little man clad in dirty white trousers and an equally dirty shirt. Behind him, fist upraised, in a furious rage and emitting lurid threats, was one of the sailors from the yacht. Immediately behind him was his mate, and, in the background, wringing his hands and expostulating vociferously, the patron.

So terrific had been the impetus given to the little man's exit that he rolled over and over, even after hitting the pavement, and fetched up against Blake's leg. Before he could scramble to his feet, the sailor was upon him, thrusting Blake aside roughly, with a snarling curse at him for being in the way. He had not had more than a vague impression of the two tramp-like individuals who had happened along at that moment. Such out-at-the-elbows persons were no novelty among the riffraff round about St. Laurent.

Before the sailor's fist could descend, he felt his arm caught in an unbreakable grip. His jaw dropped open in sheer amazement as a cold, precise voice rasped:

"That will be about enough from you, my man. Leave this fellow alone and apologise to me for being so unmannerly."

The sailor raised himself slowly and stared at the unshaven face of the man who had spoken in such unmistakable terms. The voice was that of one accustomed to be obeyed; but the scarecrow figure belied it. He made the mistake of rashly concluding that Blake and Colbert were only a couple of liberes or relegues trying to "do the heavy."

"Wot!" he roared, when his voice returned to him. "Wot are you a-sayin' of me lord duke?"

"I said, my man, that I want an apology. You have disturbed my passage along the street. That is sufficient. It will take your mind off pommelling one so much smaller than yourself."

The sailor ignored Blake sufficiently to turn his head towards where his equally astounded companion stood.

"'Ear wot the bloke says, Bill? Can you hear that so early in the mornin'? Wot'll I do to 'im? Bash 'is jore or just slap 'im on the wrist?"

His mate didn't have time to suggest which would be the better plan. His attention was brought back to the "scarecrow" in startling fashion, nothing less than a stinging blow across the face with the flat of Blake's hand.

"Perhaps that will help you to decide," he heard, in icy tones. "I'm going to teach you a lesson in manners, my man."

THE burly sailor needed no further invitation. With a roar of anticipation he straightened himself, doubled his fists, and came in with definite purpose. The little man who had been thrown out was now forgotten. He had withdrawn to a safe spot and stood watching. Colbert had already tapped his weapon to attract the second sailor's attention.

"I will fight you, each to use his right arm, if you wish. But if you interfere between the other two I will put a bullet into your leg."

"I don't fight cripples." snorted the other. "And I don't spoil a fair fight. You second your bloke, me bucko, and I'll second mine."

"Quite satisfactory."

Their brief passage of words was made to the accompaniment of a heavy blow, which Blake got home to his opponent's body. It steadied the sailor, without doing him any real injury, and made him realise that the man who could hit like that was no half-starved ex-convict, no matter what his outer appearance might suggest. On the other hand, the privations of the last two days and nights had told on Blake severely, and had the sailor possessed any real science he would have stood little chance in a rough-and-tumble.

He made no attempt to press matters, leaving it to the sailor to rush in like a bull and flail the air while striving to get a hold. It was no difficult matter to side-step, but Blake knew that his strength would not last for any prolonged period. He wanted a knockout—and he wanted it quickly.

Time after time he feinted, inviting his antagonist to take advantage of a promising opening, and time after time the great fist slid harmlessly over his shoulder.

Tap! Tap! Tap!

Blake was placing the blows almost where he wished, but not yet had the other left himself "wide open." The claret was pouring from his nose, staining the immaculate white of his blouse. He was already a different-looking figure from the spruce follow who had rolled light-heartedly across the front a quarter of an hour before, and Blake was wondering grimly what his employer would think of him if she could see him now.

That thought sent his mind back to the time when he and Tinker had been at her mercy. He grew suddenly savage as he recalled how he had been unable to deal out what he had received, and this lent a sudden viciousness and sting to his blows that had been lacking before. So amazingly swift was the change that the sailor fell back blinking in a sort of stupid wonder; and in doing so he gave Blake just the chance he needed.

Once, twice.

A hook to the jaw and a terrific left to the solar plexus. The sailor jack-knifed and went down to stay. His mate revealed signs of ignoring Colbert's threat, but Blake lifted a hand.

"I don't recall your mate," he said quietly, "but I seem to remember you. You may not recognise me at the moment, but if you will look a little more closely you may become enlightened. I spent some days as your owner's guest, a few months ago, on board La Brise. You may get your memory to work if I mention, a certain cruise to the coast of Morocco and two 'guests' who left the yacht at Tangier. Take a look!"

With that, Blake drew off his battered hat and thrust his head forward. The sailor's uplifted hand dropped as he stared into the cold grey eyes.

"Lumme!" he gasped. "It ain't so, is it? You ain't Mr. Sexton Blake?"

"I am Sexton Blake. You can pass the information on to your employer, with my compliments. And now, if you wish to try conclusions with me, I am ready."

"Not me, guv'nor! My word, wot'll Dick say when he comes round? I believes yer, guv'nor. I remembers all right. My blinkin' oath!"

He was still muttering when he knelt beside his pal. Blake and Colbert started on again, but before they had covered half a dozen paces the little man who had been the cause of it all caught Blake by the arm.

"Is that right?" he begged. "Are you really Sexton Blake—*the*

Sexton Blake?"

Blake glanced down at him curiously, he was not a pleasant specimen for the eyes to rest upon, and until that moment Blake thought he was some stray bit of flotsam of French mixed blood. But the man's English was too correct and too unaccented for that. He was British, there could be no doubt.

"What is it you want? I am Sexton Blake, an English detective, if that is what you want to know. But I am not here in any professional capacity."

"Come with me just a little way, Mr. Blake. I'll make it worth your while. I haven't much left, but I can get something. I'm ruined, and I can't get anyone to listen to me. The commandant is entirely under the spell of that she-devil. She is playing a dangerous game, and he can't, or won't, see it. Every libere and relegue in the colony is loose with money to burn, and it's my money she gave them. Only listen to me and help me to get some of my own back and I'll do anything."

Colbert would have pushed on, but Blake drew up, his attention held by the strange jumble the little man had poured out. Was he referring to Roxane Harfield? What had she to do with this wreck of a creature? What had she to do with the fact that the liberes and relegues were foot-loose about the country? And the commandant — this talk of being infatuated with her? The she-devil —what was the fellow driving at?

Suddenly he turned to Colbert.

"You can go on if you wish. Colbert. I'm going to hear what this fellow has to say. It seems to me there have been some queer things happening in St. Laurent,"

"In that case, I'll come, too, Blake. But it strikes me this fellow is not sound mentally. He raves."

A few minutes later their strange companion was taking them through a deserted warehouse that smelt of timber, and up a narrow staircase that brought them into a small office —the small office in which this same man had sat not so many hours before, gloating over certain yellow labour vouchers.

Chapter 7.   Enter Roxane.

THE wretch whom Blake had rescued was none other than Gaston Dubois, the convict labour broker. It was a very different Dubois, however, from the domineering little rat who had counted the yellow slips and afterwards browbeaten the big half-caste.

He had a tale to tell —a long story, through which, at times, it was difficult for Blake and Colbert to guess the truth. The cloud of verbal camouflage with which Dubois adorned it confused and obscured the facts. But they listened until the end, and then, strangely enough, it was the Frenchman who put searching questions.

He seemed distinctly curious regarding one reference Dubois made to an escaped libere. It had been a casual statement, but Colbert probed it this way and that until he got a semblance of the truth. Then he dropped into odd, sudden silence. Not until that afternoon was Blake to learn the reason that lay behind his interest.

Dubois' story, boiled down to essentials, suggested that he had been carrying on his business in the ordinary way when, without warning, and for no apparent reason, the girl who owned the yacht appeared in his office with a crowd of ruffians at her heels. Without giving him a chance to defend himself they had attacked him, threatened him, and forced him to walk out of the place in the midst of half the gang, two of them pressing the muzzles of pistols against his side with a threat to blow a hole in him if he made any attempt to escape or call out. At that midday hour there were few persons about, and none whom he could have called upon even had he dared.

He had been thrust into a boat and taken out to the yacht. There he had been locked up in a cabin. Later on, he discovered that the girl had opened all his drawers and boxes and had taken therefrom every scrap of paper dealing with his business. That same night he had been dragged before her and been threatened with keelhauling unless he submitted to certain demands.

He had refused, with the result that they had begun to carry out the threat. At that, he had given in, and after torture had been forced to sign an order on one of his banking accounts for no less a sum than one million francs.

He had been kept close prisoner for several days and given the torture at regular intervals. At last he had been tossed ashore like a sack of sugar and allowed to go his own way. He found his business ruined; all his sub-agents had disappeared; liberes throughout the country were roaming far and wide with plenty of money in their pockets. No libere would sign on for any work.

Slowly he had learned that it was his money that had been put into the ex-convict's pockets. His business was gone beyond recall; he was utterly ruined in health and pocket. He had gone to the commandant with his story, but that official had refused to listen to him.

He only laughed when he was told that the girl who owned the yacht was responsible for the unrest among the liberes, and had turned angry and accused him —Dubois—of being behind it all.

Since then he had wandered aimlessly, telling his experiences and warning others. But he found himself entirely discredited in a place where, only days before, he had been a power. Time and again he had met men from the yacht, and each time it had been the same. He had protested and had been thrown into the gutter. It was the latest of these incidents that Blake had witnessed.

So much for the essentials. At the start he had made a reference to the beginning of the whole mysterious sequence of events being the escape of a libere from one of the camps along the coast. It was on this point Colbert cross-examined him so closely; and then Blake, who had been very thoughtful, shot out a question that caused Dubois to look at him in an affrighted way.

"Just who were you in Canada, Dubois?"

"Wh-what? I don't understand, Mr. Blake."

Blake clicked his tongue impatiently.

"Look here, let us understand each other. You want me to help you. I will be perfectly frank. I dare say you have been playing a beastly game here preying on those poor devils of liberes. You convict labour brokers in French Guiana are all the same. But we will pass that.

"I have personal reasons why I am interested in ferreting out the truth about the unrest among the ex-convicts, and am prepared to consider your affairs if you will be perfectly frank with me. Just to stir your memory, let me ask you what part you played in the selling swindle of the Harfield lumber property in the province of New Brunswick some years ago. There were eight of you mixed up in that, and I have met Harold Carruthers. So you must be one of the other seven. Which?"

If John Harfield himself had returned to earth and his ghost had used the words, the man at the desk could not have been more amazed. Not one whisper of the past had he allowed to creep into the story he had had to tell; not a hint of any suspicion he might have as to the net of ruin which the girl on the yacht had thrown about him. Nor had he heard anything of her activities in connection with Harold Carruthers. So far back was that old business, he had almost forgotten it. There had been so many deals of a similar nature. And here was this stranger to him and French Guiana, this expedition specialist, giving him chapter and verse from the long dead past.

THE man who now called himself Gaston Dubois found a scene of long ago rising up before him in vivid colouring. His vision showed him a straight-eyed girl with russet hair, who had, apparently, accepted as gospel the lies he and Harold Carruthers had handed out to her and her mother.

He saw the big, comfortable camp at the edge of the lake, and he sat again in the luxurious office in Montreal where he and Carruthers and others had 'cut the melon' that was the proceeds of the swindle they had practised.

So long ago, so long ago! Yet out of that dim past had come the same girl, a woman now, one of wealth and purpose, and undying desire for vengeance.

A grey cloud had come over him when she first revealed herself. But now, with Sexton Blake's cool question, he felt a chill creep to his marrow. It was the same cold voice that jerked him out of the midst of memory.

"Well, Dubois, which one of the eight were you?"

"I-I—"

Blake made an impatient gesture and rose.

"I gave you a chance. I did not ask you the right and wrong of the past. I am only concerned with the present. These happenings in St. Laurent have upset my own arrangements and those with whom I am working. One death has been caused for certain; others may have occurred before now. My friends have been placed in danger, and the preparatory work of many weeks jeopardised. It is not to be tolerated. But you can expect no assistance from me unless you tell me what I want to know. Will you come, Colbert?"

But Dubois was also on his feet. "Don't go," he cried hysterically. "I'll tell you whatever you want to know, only get some of my money back from that she-devil. Whatever I did in the past didn't deserve what she has done to me. Your friend is interested in the libere who escaped. I can tell you more about him, too. Don't go!"

Blake gazed down at him with contempt.

"You are a poor specimen, Dubois, but sometimes we have to employ untempered tools. Sit down!"

The broker obeyed. Blake also dropped back into his seat and lit a cigarette.

"I ask you once more," he said wearily. "Which one of the eight are you?"

"My name is Henley,"

"Chris Henley?"

"Yes."

"If I remember rightly, it was you who took a leading part with Harold Carruthers in the swindle."

"We were all equal, but it was Carruthers and I who went down to the camp."

"Quite so. How did Miss Harfield discover you were operating here in St. Laurent under the name of Gaston Dubois?"

"I can't guess. She has devoted years to this idea of hers and I suppose has built up a system of inquiry!"

"She has given proof of that," commented Blake dryly. "But we will disregard the ethics of what happened in the past just for the present. Whatever it was, two wrongs don't make a right, and the girl is playing with fire in setting these ex-convicts loose with money in their pockets. I should say she has ruined your business beyond repair, Henley."

He groaned.

"It is gone for ever. Government will have shooting trouble on their hands before this business is over. Then they will make a clean-up and take all the labour control into their own hands. Favre is a fool. He won't listen to anyone but the girl."

"Never mind that. Let us got down to brass tacks. Now listen!"

Blake drew his chair closer and began to talk, asking many questions to which Henley replied as truthfully as possible. When Blake had finished Colbert took up the ball, probing still more deeply into the affair of the escaped libere who was hidden, so Henley insisted, on board the yacht.

"Does the commandant know of this?" was Colbert's final query.

"He wouldn't let me tell him. He must be in her pay. I don't suppose anyone else here knows."

"Then let me warn you to say nothing more about it. Do you understand?"

"Yes; I will keep mum if Mr. Blake will help me to recover some of my money."

The attention of the three men in the tiny office was caught by a sudden rhythmic sound on the boarded floor beneath. Men swinging along in step —an unmistakable heat. Then the nearer approach and a somewhat shorter tempo that told them a disciplined party of men were mounting the stairs.

Chris Henley's eyes were full of fear as he stared towards the door. Blake and Colbert displayed cool interest. Then, without ceremony, the door was drawn open and the three pairs of eyes became riveted on —Roxane Harfield.

SHE was dressed just as they had seen her an hour ago or so before, all in fresh white with a sun hat crowning her russet hair. Behind her loomed two white-bloused sailors, the front of the double file that had followed her up the stairs.

They had halted at a curt word from their mistress and now remained as expressionless as wood.

Through the shallow waves of smoke in the room she shot one contemptuous glance at the broker; another quick look of appraisal she gave to Professor Colbert; and then her eyes swung to Sexton Blake. Smouldering anger showed in their depths as she gazed upon the ragged, unshaven figure that she had never before seen other than perfectly groomed.

"So I have not been misinformed," she said quietly, in the low, husky tones that Blake remembered so well.

Blake had risen, not so much out of courtesy as from a desire to be on his feet in case anything "broke." He bowed ironically.

"If you mean about my presence in St. Laurent, that is quite correct, Miss Harfield."

The words were empty. Blake was thinking fast, as was Colbert.

Both men sensed the menace of the girl's sudden appearance with a bunch of men from the yacht at her heels.

Colbert didn't know the situation between Roxane Harfield, Carruthers, Henley, and the other six men who had played a part in the swindle of years ago. Nor could he and Blake put an exact estimate on Henley's wild statements regarding the infatuation of the commandant for the girl.

On the other hand, there was the commandant's unsatisfactory letter to Colonel Favres; there was the undoubted fact that a great unrest was spreading among the liberes; there was the unmistakable fact that Chris Henley had been ruined with efficiency and despatch; and there was the sight they had witnessed with their own eyes of the girl taking her morning drive in the commandant's carriage. And now she certainly seemed to be carrying matters with a high hand.

It was obvious that she had returned from the drive and heard what had happened between Blake and the sailor; and it was equally plain that she had lost no time in getting together a sufficient number of her men to take matters into her own hands.

But what else might lie behind this boldness was not yet plain. It was the curl of her lip and sudden movement to one side that put Blake and Colbert even more on guard.

"Watch, Colbert," said Blake quietly, "mademoiselle intends mischief!"

She laughed shortly.

"There are several things to be reckoned between us, Mr. Meddlesome Blake. Not least is your palaver with that miserable creature beside you."

Suddenly she brought from the folds of her skirt a short whip which, until that moment, they had not seen. She gripped it as she scorned Chris Henley.

"I warned you to leave the town and not return," she said in tones that vibrated with hate. "You have disobeyed that order. When I have settled with these two interfering busy-bodies I shall whip you within an inch of your life. I'll break you completely this time, Chris Henley."

"Mademoiselle!"

It was Colbert who interrupted. His face was stern, his voice imperative.

"I would have you remember that you are threatening two members of an official expedition," he went on. "I am Professor Colbert, of the University of Paris, and an unofficial member of Government. It will be my painful duty to request Colonel Favre to curtail your liberties in St. Laurent. I demand that you withdraw your men, and permit me and my friend, Monsieur Blake, to pass out. We have undergone severe privations during the past two days and are both wounded. What differences you may have can be settled at another time and in another way."

Roxane had been listening with apparently close attention; but now she laughed, low and mockingly.

"It pains me, monsieur," she answered, "but I am afraid I shall be unable to wait for Colonel Favre. We will settle our differences in a place where we shall be undisturbed."

With that she stepped still further to one side so that she was almost shrouded in the dusk of the hall. Then they heard her voice once more, husky and tense.

"Attention, men. Bring them out!"

She watched while Blake,
held safely by four of her
sailors, was hauled out from
the corner. "Take him to
the boat," she ordered.

Chapter 8.   Roxane's Trick.

NO more warning was needed than that.

Blake didn't know just how many men were in the press in the hall, but he knew that the odds would be heavy enough against him and Colbert, not counting the added handicap of the professor's wounded arm and his own crocked leg. Henley was out of consideration as an asset.

His automatic was out, and he was shooting by the time the first of the sailors mobbed through the narrow doorway. He shot low, and with definite purpose, sending two men down before those behind could scramble over the prone forms.

But even in that brief space of time Blake found cause for amazement, and an upsurging feeling akin to anger. Instead of the Frenchman whipping out his weapon and doing as much damage as he could, he had folded his arms, and was standing quietly, waiting to be seized.

As for Henley he had given one frightened squeal at the first signs of onslaught, and then took a header clean through the Venetian blinds, landing on the roof of a small lean-to building outside. Down this he rolled and dropped to the ground.

Thus, left alone, Blake met the rush as best he could. When it was useless to attempt to keep on shooting he used his weapon as a club, and when that did not avail he used his fists, edging himself into one corner where not more than two of his assailants could reach him at once.

He would have needed to be more than a superman to withstand the weight that hemmed him in. There were few weaklings among the crew of La Brise, and certainly none among those Roxane had chosen for the present purpose in hand.

By sheer weight they forced him to his knees, hammered him to the floor, and arm-locked him, so he was helpless. None could tell what thoughts might be passing in Roxane's mind.

After one quick, puzzled glance at Colbert, when he surrendered gracefully, she had eyes only for the struggle in the corner. Henley she seemed to dismiss as of no account from the moment he dived through the window.

Yet there was nothing of triumph in her manner as she watched while Blake, held safely by four of the battered sailors, was hauled out from the corner and on to his feet.

"Take him to the boat," she ordered curtly. "Get across the front as quickly us possible." Then she turned to the professor. "You will come quietly?"

"Mademoiselle, what else is there to do but to surrender to superior force? I shall give no trouble."

Something like contempt flashed in her eyes, but she only shrugged.

"You will walk between two of my men, then. Ready! Let us get on!"

The sailors fell into double line again, those who were able to walk, and with Blake held securely, while Professor Colbert obediently walked next, they started down the stairs, leaving three of their number to assist the wounded.

The stairs leading up to the small office mounted from the main warehouse where, under normal conditions, mahogany would be piled, waiting to be shipped. At the present time there were only a few odd scraps of timber in the place, for Henley had not been operating to any extent for some time.

The great shed was gloomy, odorous of sawn wood, and almost in darkness, the wooden shutters being closed and light coming only through one of the big swing doors that gave on to the quay. On the stairs and the floor beneath the measured tramp of Roxane's men sounded in hollow echo.

Outside, the sun beat down in naked glare. One slouching figure could be seen through the oblong opening; beyond that solitary negro the town seemed still to be sunk in siesta.

Then it seemed as if the very cobbles came to life. From every side they came pressing forward towards the opening in the warehouse, grinning savagely, cursing, sweating, herding forward. A grotesque little figure that danced among them urged them with profane promises.

For a moment the sailors paused in sheer stupefaction at the sight. Coming down the stairs, Roxane saw, at first, only a blurred mass at the door. Then she discerned the identity of the one who urged them on. It was Chris Henley.

Whatever the extent of his physical cowardice, Henley's mind had been functioning at high pressure. He knew that he had one hope, and one hope only, of retrieving his fortunes; that was through Sexton

Blake.

It didn't matter two pins to him what Blake's opinion of the ethics of the matter might be. Blake had been put to serious inconvenience by the recklessness with which Roxane had stirred up the ex-convict liberes. It suited Blake's purpose, for the time being, to use Henley, and it suited Henley to lean on Blake. Therefore, his first thought had been as he dived through the window, that in some way he must rescue Blake.

Roxane had forced out of him a great slice of the money he had hoarded, but she had not got it all. He could still command several thousand francs, and in this moment of desperation he gambled it in the hope that he would get it back many times over—through Sexton Blake.

At that hour of the day there were plenty of desperate characters to be found in the back room of the Cafe Napoleon, and other wine shops along the front. What they had received of his—Henley's—money through Roxane was spent long ago. Their allegiance belonged to whoever showed the colour of more money. And, moreover, they knew "Gaston Dubois" as one who could pay if need be.

Hence there were many ears to listen as the ex-broker dashed into the cafe, offering money here, promising rich reward there if they would do his bidding. And there wasn't any love lost between the riff-raff of the port and the sailors in spotless uniform, who swaggered a bit when they passed through the town.

From the Cafe Napoleon to the next wine shop, and the next, Henley flew, until he had collected half a hundred of as savage rascals as could be raked up in St. Laurent du Maroni.

For weapons they had staves, knives, and one or two revolvers. Some half-dozen carried machetes. With Henley screaming his orders, they poured forth, as villainous a rabble as one could get together. And this it was that Roxane saw as she reached the foot of the stairs. Sexton Blake saw it, too—saw it, and wondered how Henley had managed the trick —wondered what would be the outcome.

FOR the barest moment Roxane hesitated. Despite the power she had gained over Colonel Favre, she knew perfectly well that she could not set the whole town by the ears without the official guard being brought into action. To beguile the commandant was one thing; to clash with the police was another.

It had been her plan to get hold of Blake before any real upheaval could be created, and she had counted on being able to bamboozle the commandant once she had her prisoner aboard the yacht. And then, if things became too hot, she would slip away to sea.

Now she saw but one thing for it —to fight through the mob and reach the boat. But she would not yield her prisoners until she was forced to it.

"Go through them, men," she called sharply. "Get your prisoners aboard and return with reinforcements. I will hold the room upstairs with our wounded!"

She stood watching while the sailors closed in and then, with a yell, rushed forward, attempting to wedge their way through. Inflamed by Henley's shouts and promises, the liberes met them in a snarling pack. The melee broke in two ways, part of it exploding on to the front where, a wedge of Roxane's men drove through; the rest reeling back in a confused mass into the dimness of the warehouse.

Blake found himself free. Every hand was needed to stem the tide of that pack. He had lost sight of Colbert. But his hands were free once more, and that was all that mattered.

Chris Henley had been right in his calculations. At that moment Blake was determined to cut the ground out from under Roxane's feet if possible. Their final reckoning could be governed by circumstances. Just now he had his own job to look after, and that meant the relief of the little expedition isolated in the jungle.

He found himself in an inextricable tangle against the wall. He laid about him with more than a will, for he was not forgetting how he had been overborne in the room above. Slowly but inevitably Roxane's men gave way. Separated, they could not withstand the overwhelming numbers. From the stairs, Roxane urged them to rally after rally and, at one moment, Blake saw her draw her automatic as if she would begin to shoot.

But before this happened another factor appeared on the scene. Through the struggling mass outside drove half a dozen uniformed guards; high above the uproar sounded the short, sharp command of a young officer.

Lieutenant Cambon, escorting a score of convicts to the quayside for transhipment to Devil's Island, had seen the strange sight at the entrance to the warehouse. Leaving half his men in charge of the convict party, he had come to investigate.

He knew perfectly well the spell the beautiful girl on the yacht had cast over his superior; but duty was duty with him, and he had seen more of the unrest among the liberes than the commandant would acknowledge existed.

Before those uniforms the riff-raff broke and fled. Those outside sped along the quay as fast as their legs would carry them. Those inside needed but the sight of the dreaded uniforms to throw them into a panic. Like frightened rats they dashed this way and that. Being wise in his generation, the young officer allowed them to go.

When none but Roxane and her party remained, with Blake and Colbert standing at one side, Lieutenant Cambon made punctilious request for information. Chris Henley was not there to make answer. Only Roxane spoke, to carry things with a high hand.

The officer listened politely.

"These gentlemen," he said, glancing towards Blake and the professor, "what part have they in this trouble?"

Professor Colbert stepped forward and revealed his identity. In the face of that Lieutenant Cambon stiffened. He knew that the professor was a member of the Franco-British Expedition, and knew him as a man of power and influence in France. It were better to go easy here.

"I shall report the matter to Colonel Favre," he said stiffly. "Mademoiselle, it will be better if you will withdraw your men, I shall communicate to you what decision Colonel Favre makes in this matter."

And, in the face of that, Roxane could do nothing but obey.

IN the room at the hotel which they reached considerably later than they had intended, Blake learned why Professor Colbert had acted in such strange fashion in the warehouse.

"It was because I saw a chance to get on board the yacht without rousing suspicion," he confided. "I knew that you must think me cowardly, my friend, but it was what that rascally broker said that influenced me. It was not only for the sake of the expedition that I came to this benighted place; that was a means to an end. You heard what Dubois said about the libere whom this adventuress rescued from the sea? He was my reason. There is a story of the past there, my friend. I will tell it to you. If he is the same whom I seek, then my search is ended."

After a pause he related to the detective the story that had had its beginning years before; a tale of intrigue within intrigue in which the victim had been carefully chosen and such a case built up against him that there was not a loophole of escape.

"It was the plot of a jealous man," Blake heard him saying in one of the periods of explanation. "He was rich and powerful, and yet it was my brother, a poor, struggling physician, who won the heart of the girl. With infinite cunning this fiend laid his plans; with the most diabolical cunning did he carry out the murder. Yet the evidence was all against my brother.

"I possessed influence enough to have the major sentence commuted to one of penal servitude, and ever since that day I have worked to gain his pardon and release. That villain, however, is still a power in the land, it has been a long and silent battle between us, Blake.

"Sometimes I have gained a trick; at other times he has. I hoped to achieve victory by coming out here. I have brought with me certain papers from strong sources in France. But I was anticipated. It was arranged that my brother should be sent to one of the camps in the forest and there meet a slow death through privation. You and I know, my friend, what a few days of that life can do to a man. But Fate intervened in the person of this young woman. I can forgive all that we have gone through, and disregard the pot she has set boiling in this country, if I can see my brother go free. But I had to know. Once aboard the yacht I should have discovered if it were really he. But now—"

Blake was sympathetic. On the other hand he was not forgetting that he, too, owed a duty. Back in the jungle were his friends, needing early succour; and roaming about the land were the bands of liberes, inflamed by their new-found economic freedom and made arrogant by the handling of such sums of money as they had not before seen. It was irony that it should be Chris Henley's money that was causing the mischief.

"I quite see your point, Colbert." he conceded. "But there are other things to be considered. If that is your brother I shall gladly do what I can to get him away out of French jurisdiction. Let him remain on board the yacht. But this girl must be brought up sharp.

"It strikes me that after what happened this morning she will make a quick move of some kind. She must realise that we are in a position to place before Colonel Favre such evidence as he must consider, no matter how infatuated he may be with her, or even if, as Henley suggested, he is in her pay.

"If we had been taken aboard the yacht there would have been a delay that might have been fatal to our comrades in the forest. When my mind is easy on that score I care not what she does.

"And I am not forgetting that, whatever his faults, we owe our freedom at this moment to the quickness of Gaston Dubois in collecting that gang of ruffians to try to rescue us. I think we should seek an interview with the commandant as early as possible."

"I shall dispatch a note at once, my friend, for what you say is true," replied the Frenchman.

IT was late in the hour of siesta by the time Professor Colbert had written his note to the commandant and dispatched it by one of the hotel negroes.

Neither he nor Blake bothered to indulge in the custom that put the whole town asleep during those two hours of the day; nor did they find any cause for surprise in the fact that the messenger did not return, though the early afternoon dragged on towards the cooler hours.

Stretched out on the back veranda, overlooking a cool patio, they were content enough to take things easy for the time being. And it was just because of this that they were not witnesses of what was proceeding on the water-front. It was none other than Gaston Dubois, or rather Chris Henley, who brought them news which Blake found disturbing.

He came, a slinking figure of furtive mien, and, looking at him, Blake had to confess to himself that Roxane had certainly accomplished what she had set out to do.

"It will be too late if you do not move soon," he almost whispered. "The yacht will be gone."

Blake sat up with a jerk.

"Gone! What do you mean?"

"You can see for yourself. There are signs that she is getting ready to put to sea. I have seen a big lighter of stores being unloaded. And that she-devil has just driven away from the quay. I'll bet she's going to see the commandant."

It was this announcement that stirred Colbert.

"Was she alone?"

"Yes—in a hired carriage. But she will be back soon, you will see. She will get Favre to fix her papers with his own hand, and then there will be nothing to stop her."

"And we sent our note more than an hour ago," mused Blake. "What do you say, Colbert?"

"Do as you think best, Blake. I don't care what happens so long as that other person gets away."

"But my money!" wailed Henley.

"Shut up!" snapped Blake. "You are lucky you are not in a gang in the forest. But let me think. I want a final word with that girl. Colbert, and I'm going to get it. Here, you, Henley, we can depend on you in this. You daren't go to the commandant's house, but you can find someone you can trust. Send him along there on the double-quick, and discover what has become of our messenger. Then report here."

Nothing loath, the broker made off, promising fervently to report shortly. Colbert would not leave his chair, but Blake walked through to the front gallery overlooking the water-front, and gazed out to where the yacht lay at anchor. A few moments' scrutiny sufficed to show him that Henley was not mistaken. A big lighter was even then being unloaded, and there were other definite signs that preparations were being made to leave.

IF Blake could have entered Colonel Favre's big, private bureau at that moment he would have understood why the first messenger sent with Colbert's letter had not returned. He had expected some definite move on Roxane's part in order to counteract the unfavourable impression her high-handed action at the warehouse had made on the young officer.

But he had hardly anticipated she would carry out as bold a plan as she was even now putting into effect, for the simple reason that he had no means of knowing how completely she had infatuated the susceptible commandant.

So certain was she of her powers that she had given her orders for departure before dashing to the administrator's house. She did not expect to be kept waiting; nor was she. Favre, naturally weak where women were concerned, was ripe for the net cast by such a lovely creature as Roxane Harfield, who, into that pestiferous hole, had come as a breath of loveliness to which he had long been a stranger.

Duty, honour—everything had been subordinated to the consuming desire she had roused in him; and had she but said the word, it would have found him ready to accompany her in the yacht, to throw overboard for her sake promotion, retirement, pension, or any other fruits of office. In fact, he had been giving the idea of flight with her more and more serious consideration. And Roxane had sensed this.

She knew that she must get hold of the situation and control it until she was ready to leave. Even Favre could hardly refuse to hear the report of the young officer if he were admitted. She must prevent that, and she must put a spoke in Sexton Blake's wheel. She knew only too well it would be disastrous to her plans if he once got a grip of the actual situation.

Favre received her in the privacy of his big private room, where he had been making a pretence of going through some papers.

She moved close to him and laid one slim hand on his pudgy fist, repressing the feeling of distaste that overwhelmed her at the touch. It wasn't the first time that the girl had found it difficult to play her part, and only her unbreakable determination to carry out the vow she had made had enabled her to go through with the game of duplicity.

Yet on this day she felt a greater repulsion than ever; but only she knew it was because Sexton Blake was so close to her. The vision of that grim, ragged, limping, careworn man had brought music into her soul that she might resist with all her strength, that she might try to ignore, that she might flee from, but that she could not deny.

Yet she would not yield; she would fight to the last and beat him, finding pain and joy at the same time in doing so. And for these reasons her allure for Favre was all the more devastating as her soft, husky voice fell seductively on his ears.

"Enemies of mine have arrived in St. Laurent du Maroni," she said plaintively "I have come to the one I know I can trust."

His free hand went up and touched her.

"You know you can command me, mademoiselle," he said thickly. "I would do anything for you—I would even cast aside everything and go away with you."

"Would you come this day if I asked it?"

"Yes—this moment."

"I may ask that before the day is done. But there are many things to think of first. We should have to be careful. But if I should, you will do a little thing for me?"

"You know it."

"There is an Englishman here who would hinder me. His name is Sexton Blake. He is a member of an expedition that has been in the interior: You know of it, for they must have had your permission. Will you refuse to see him and his companion—one of your own countrymen, a Professor Colbert?"

"Yes—for you."

"And some of my men have had a little trouble with one of your young officers. He may blame them. Will you refuse to see anyone—everyone—until later in the day?"

"I will give orders now."

"You are good and strong," she murmured.

Favre patted her hand fatuously and struck his bell. Roxane got up swiftly and walked to the other side of the room, where she made pretence of studying a map on the wall. She was still there when an orderly entered to receive the commandant's orders that he was not to be approached on any pretext during the rest of the day unless he should ring.

When the man was gone he turned to Roxane, his eyes humid with the desire that filled him.

"Have I proved my words, mademoiselle?"

She approached him again, sitting on the arm his chair. He was now in a state of such complete surrender that the girl could have wrung any favour she wished had she willed. Again his podgy hand touched the slim curve of her body, causing her to shudder as if it were cold. But she only smiled and allowed her arm to pass lightly across his fat shoulders until her fingers were hovering close to the thick, red roll at the back of his neck

Then—

Into the flesh she jabbed the point of a hypodermic needle that she had got ready while pretending to find interest in the map on the wall. And over the wide mahogany of the desk slumped Colonel Favre—just as, some time before, Sexton Blake had collapsed upon the wheel of the Grey Panther in London with a shot of the same dope benumbing his senses.

Then the girl slid off the chair, looked for a moment at her victim, and this time laid a hand on his shoulder that brought her no shudder of distaste.

"I'm sorry I had to make such a fool of you." she whispered. "I hope you won't have to pay too big a price. You were a cog in the machine, and it had to be."

She stole to the big windows that gave out on to the wide veranda and thence to the garden, by which she could reach the spot where the carriage waited. Just before passing out she paused once more and gazed back. But this time her eyes were hard and mocking.

"Crack that nut if you can, Sexton Blake!" she muttered.

Then she was gone, a filmy bit of white floating along through the exotic colour in the garden.

AGAIN and again that day Sexton Blake made strenuous efforts to gain entry to Colonel Favre. But he might as well have kept hanging his head against a brick wall with as little profit. No one—not even the officer of the day—dared penetrate to that private bureau in face of the commandant's explicit orders.

And when, later in the day, he saw the white yacht move slowly out of harbour with a mocking flutter of the burgee of the Royal Canadian Yacht Club, Blake bit on the end of his pipe savagely.

"Hanged if you haven't made it trick and game!" he muttered. "I don't know just what last card you played, but you've diddled us neatly. I'll find the explanation when I get through to that poor fish, Favre; but there are fifty-two cards in every pack, and they aren't all dealt yet."

But, for once, Sexton Blake could do naught but stand by and wait until enlightenment came from another source; and it was some hours after that when Colonel Favre struggled back to consciousness and bitter realisation through the fogged state into which he had plunged at the touch of that hypodermic needle.

Nor was it any consolation to Blake that the arrival of a French cruiser nipped in the bud the unrest among the liberes and relegues that was threatening to grow into one of the most dangerous outbreaks that the penal settlement had over known.

It did not assist Blake that a puzzled governor at Cayenne made short work of Favre when he learned a hint of the truth. Blake was too deeply chagrined over his failure to bring to book the girl who, for her own private purposes, had thrown the whole country into a turmoil, and placed in jeopardy the little party of scientists back in the forest.

He had no blame for Colbert in the latter's joy at his brother's escape. He knew that Roxane would see that the poor devil found an asylum where he would never again be in danger from the intrigues that had sapped so much of his life. He could even find it in his heart to be grateful to Roxane for that.

But during the next two weeks, when he struggled back to the camp with a scratch lot of bearers who were only held in leash by the menace of that glim, grey cruiser, he vowed that the day must come when Roxane should pay a heavy price for her victory.

THE END.
[24700 WORDS, NOVELETTE]

OTHER CONTENTS INCLUDE: 'CRIMES THAT THRILLED THE WORLD'; AND THE CONTINUING SERIAL 'THE ADVENTURES OF RALPH RASHLEIGH'.

'Crimes that Thrilled the World' in this issue offered up the conclusion to the 'Curiosity' murder which was a sensational murder at that time. It was committed in Chicago, and the defendents, who plead guilty, were defended, in sentencing, by Clarence Darrow.

Unfortunately, this copy of the story could not be properly digitized, else I would have presented it. A summary can be found in Wikipedia.

/drf